Code Red at the Supermall

A Tom & Liz Austen Mystery

by

ERIC WILSON

ORCA BOOK PUBLISHERS

As in his other mysteries, Eric Wilson writes here about imaginary people in a real landscape.

Find Eric Wilson at www.ericwilson.com

For information: Orca Book Publishers, PO Box 468, Custer, WA, USA, 98240-0468.

http://www.orcabook.com

First published in hardcover by Collins Publishers, 1988
First US edition by Orca Book Publishers, 2000

Canadian Cataloguing in Publication Data
Wilson, Eric.
  Code red at the supermall

  ISBN 1-55143-172-6

  I. Title.
PS8595.I583C62 2000   jC813'.54   C99-911075-6
PZ7.W6935Co 2000

Library of Congress Catalog Card Number: 99-067402

01 00 99   5 4 3 2 1

Printed and bound in the United States

cover design: *Richard Bingham*
cover and chaper illustrations: *Richard Row*
logo photograph: *Lawrence McLagan*

For my niece Julia Wilson,
so new to our world.
And my friend Stuart Buchan,
gone much too soon.

THE INDOOR SEA

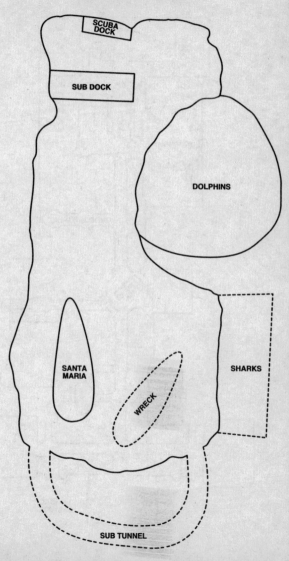

WEST EDMONTON MALL

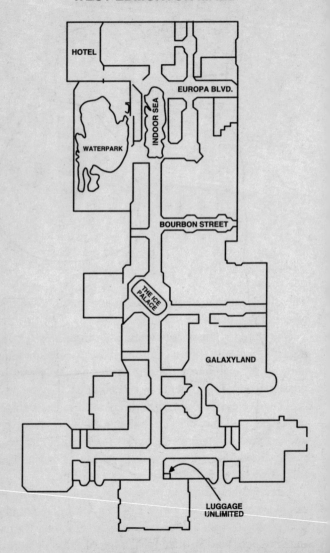

1

The shark came out of the darkness, moving swiftly toward Liz Austen.

She stared at the deadly teeth and stepped back with a gasp. As the shark reached the glass wall of its tank and swept away, Liz glanced at the people standing nearby, wondering if her fear was obvious.

They were all in a dark underground cave. Behind one glass wall the sharks circled in their big tank; on another side of the cave penguins preened themselves, while crocodiles with gleaming yellow eyes watched their visitors.

Leaving the cave, Liz hurried up some stairs to the marble corridors of the West Edmonton Mall. Sunlight poured down from domed windows high above, warming shoppers who strolled past some of the 828 stores.

The sun sparkled on the blue water of an indoor sea where subs moved slowly past a Spanish galleon, lighting up the dolphins performing spectacular leaps in their pool beside the sea.

Behind a high glass wall was the World Waterpark, where girls and boys strolled on a beach under palm trees, kids surfed the big waves and others plunged down an amazing collection of waterslides that were intertwined like green and blue snakes.

Nearby, Liz saw a store called Lots of Fun Stuff. It featured a display of stick-on tattoos, which the owner explained were very realistic. "They'll come off, of course, but you need to follow my special, printed instructions."

"I like the bats," Liz said. "Their eyes are really scary."

Consulting her map of the mall, Liz decided to visit Bourbon Street, a replica of the famous tourist attraction in New Orleans. It featured restaurants like the Café Orleans facing a street of cobblestones and benches. Lights twinkled above suggesting a night sky, neon signs glowed outside the restaurants, and realistic mannequins stood on second-floor balconies above the crowds parading past.

A girl named Susan waited for customers at a row of old-fashioned shoeshine chairs. Like Liz, she was 16. "The money's good and it's a great summer job," Susan laughed, "but sometimes I get homesick for Nova Scotia."

"I miss home, but I sure love this place."

"How much longer are you staying?"

"Until this weekend. My Dad's teaching a course to the mall's security guards. After that," Liz pouted, "we fly home."

"Did you say he's an inspector in the Winnipeg police?"

"That's right. He's . . ."

"Liz, something's wrong!"

"What do you mean?"

"Listen!"

From speakers hidden in the ceiling, an urgent voice was saying, "*Code Red, Bourbon Street. Code Red, Bourbon Street.*" Susan quickly put away her brushes and polishes. "Code Red is the maximum alert for security guards. There's some kind of trouble here in Bourbon Street."

Liz looked at the people strolling past. "Who's going to tell them?"

"The guards will be here any second and they'll clear everyone from the area."

"But what about the Code Red? We won't know what it's about!" Liz stepped closer to Susan. "I have to find out what happened. Is there anywhere I could hide?"

Susan hesitated, then looked at a nearby booth. It was decorated with the signs of the zodiac, and the promise to reveal your *past, present and future.* "The fortune-teller's away and she left me her key. You could hide in there."

"Great!" Liz saw security guards at the entrance to Bourbon Street asking people to leave. "Hurry, Susan, hurry." Then, safely inside the booth, she called from the darkness, "Thanks a million! See you tomorrow."

"Let's hope so."

Crouching against the wooden wall, Liz listened to the guards clearing people from the area. As the Code Red continued to sound, a curious hush fell over

Bourbon Street. A few minutes later Liz's heart skipped when she heard her father's voice saying as he approached, "A package?"

"Yes, Inspector Austen," someone replied. "We've alerted the local police, but we'd like you to take a look right away."

"The robot can't get up there?"

"No, sir. Whoever planted this thing made sure a robot couldn't get near it."

As the voices faded away, Liz slowly raised her eyes to a crack in the wall. Through it she saw neon lights glowing along the street, now deserted except for several security guards. They stood in the distance with arms crossed and faces creased into frowns as they watched her father step onto the balcony above the Café Orleans.

Kneeling, he cautiously reached toward a package wrapped in brown paper. Liz was certain it was a bomb.

2

Moments later several police officers ran into the Café Orleans, just as Mr. Austen stood up from the package, a smile of relief on his face. The situation looked under control, so Liz raced from the booth and up the restaurant stairs. Grabbing her father, she hugged him. "Are you okay, Dad? Can I help you?"

"Liz, how did you . . . ?"

"I'll tell you later, okay?" She looked at the police officers studying the package. "How'd the security guards learn about the bomb?"

"An anonymous tip over the phone."

"A man or a woman?"

"Impossible to say. The caller's voice was deliberately muffled."

"Didn't they leave a note beside that thing? Demanding a ransom or something?"

"Nothing."

"Why do you think it was planted on the balcony?"

"Normally a robot would be used to investigate the bomb, so there'd be no risk to anyone. Whoever left that bomb wanted to make sure that the robot couldn't be used."

"So that's a real bomb? Not a fake?"

"It's the real thing all right, but there's one unusual thing about it. A key wire wasn't connected. I realized right away that someone was sending a serious message by planting this bomb."

"What do you mean?"

"One message: This person's an expert because that's a sophisticated device. The bomber's saying that, for now, no one's going to get hurt. But we can expect there will be more trouble, probably with minimum danger at first. The bomber's motive may be to hurt the mall without firing a shot. I'm only guessing, of course, but we've certainly got a strange character on our hands."

* * *

Just then a tall woman with the striking eyes and high cheekbones of the Cree Indians approached. She smiled as Liz was introduced by her father. "Cathy Winter Eagle, meet my daughter. I'm very proud of Liz and her brother Tom."

Liz hugged her Dad. He was tall and handsome, with black hair and eyes, and she was proud of him, too. "Pleased to meet you, Inspector Winter Eagle."

"Inspector? I'm impressed you noticed."

"Your uniform has the same number of pips as my Dad's."

As the pair discussed the case, Liz glanced around the restaurant's upper floor, wondering how the bomb had been smuggled onto the balcony. The entire floor was empty, and there was no trace of whoever had planted the bomb. For a moment she looked at a grill in the wall, enjoying the feel of the cool air that blew through it. There was a door right beside it, but when she tried the handle it was locked.

Back downstairs, after they had left Bourbon Street, Liz asked her father what would happen next.

"Cathy will use the police computer to search out names of previous mall employees who've been fired, also any troublemakers who've been banned from the premises." He looked at the inspector. "Have you got a few minutes? I'd like you to meet my wife."

She looked at the officers who'd begun fingerprinting the scene. "They'll be busy for a while, so that's a good idea."

Still talking about the incident, the trio made the long walk through the gigantic mall to the hotel at its far end. "My room's really fabulous," Liz said to Inspector Winter Eagle. "Do you want to come and see it on the way to my Mom and Dad's suite?"

"Certainly."

The elevator came to a stop and the doors opened. They stepped into a corridor with dark mirrors and a red HOLLYWOOD sign. In Liz's room neon stars glowed on walls blacker than ebony and tiny lights twinkled in the deep-purple carpet. "Those are fibre optics," Liz explained. "Neat, eh?"

"You bet."

On another floor they entered a marbled hallway lined with pillars. The word ROME was in gold letters on the wall, backlit by a soft red glow.

"I've heard of this hotel's theme rooms," Inspector Winter Eagle remarked to Liz, "but I didn't know the hallways are also themed to fit the rooms."

"On the Polynesian floor, the rooms have Jacuzzis with volcanoes beside them that actually belch steam!"

Mr. Austen opened a door at the end of the hallway. "We're here as guests of the mall while I'm teaching a course to the security personnel. My son's friend Dietmar came with us, too."

The inspector gazed at the thick carpet's rich burgundy colour, which was repeated in the spread that covered a round bed enclosed by sheer curtains. Nearby, potted plants hung above the huge marble tub. Beside it was a statue of a Roman serving maid, in her hand a golden spout through which water plunged when the bath was filled.

Mrs. Austen was working at a desk. She was tall with blue eyes, and had hair the colour of flames. "Ted's told me lots about you, Cathy, so I'm glad we're finally able to meet," she said to the inspector with a warm smile.

Suddenly the hallway door opened and Liz saw her brother, and a second boy of about the same age. "Uh oh—here comes trouble in the form of Dietmar Oban. When you shake hands with him, Inspector, beware of him greeting you with a hand-buzzer."

"He looks nice."

"Appearances can be deceiving."

Tom was tall for 14. Like his mother, his hair was red, his eyes blue. Dietmar was shorter and rounder, with brown hair and eyes to match. He seemed excited about something, so Liz watched him warily as Mr. Austen poured refreshments into glasses. Then she got distracted by the conversation about what the bomber's motives could be. As the others discussed various possibilities, Liz took a sip of bubbly spring water and then almost choked when she saw a fly in the glass. She screamed and the glass dropped from her hand, then Dietmar sprang forward to retrieve the plastic fly.

"So that's where I left the little devil."

"Tom Austen," Liz said, as the others chuckled. "If you invite this odious creature on any more holidays, you can count me out."

Smiling, Inspector Winter Eagle looked at her watch. "I'd better get back to that bomb investigation. They'll be finishing off the preliminary stuff—picture taking, dusting for fingerprints—so I can really get started on my investigation." A beep sounded from her belt, followed by a static-filled voice speaking in police codes. "There's a problem at one of the mall's stores. It's probably not connected with the bomb incident, but I'd better check."

"May we come?" Tom asked.

"Sure."

Soon everyone but Dietmar was descending in the elevator. "That guy," Tom laughed. "Can you believe he'd rather watch TV than witness a police investigation? He's such a couch potato I could probably sell him to McDonald's." Then, as the doors opened onto the lobby he added, "But he's fun with that weird sense of humour."

"He's different," Liz said. "I'll sure admit that."

In the mall, neon store signs were reflected on the green surface of the indoor sea. Surrounded by a rocky shoreline and the brightly lit stores, the sea was dominated by the *Santa Maria*, a replica of the galleon that carried Christopher Columbus to the New World.

"People aren't allowed on the *Santa Maria*," Liz said. "It's a real ship that was made in British Columbia, and then shipped here in pieces and rebuilt. But there's nothing inside except a huge tank of tropical fish."

"Have you been on board to see them?"

"No, some kids in the mall gave me that scoop."

"Why the fish if nobody's allowed on the *Santa Maria*?" Mr. Austen asked.

"Because of the submarines." Liz pointed at a yellow conning tower rising above the surface. The vessel was creating small waves as it slowly moved forward through the water. "Those are real subs. The trip goes around the edge of the sea and passengers look out the portholes at all kinds of tropical fish in underwater tanks."

"Plus the ruins of the lost civilization of Atlantis," Tom added. "It's totally realistic."

"Where does that tunnel go?" Mrs. Austen pointed at a dark opening in the rocky wall surrounding the sea.

"That's how the subs change direction," Tom replied. "They go into the tunnel, make a loop and come out that portal below us."

"I'm dying to see inside the tunnel," Liz said, "but it's out of bounds for visitors." She looked down at a flipper-footed figure in scuba gear swimming silently among the underwater plants of the indoor sea. "Wouldn't that be fun?"

"Say, we'd better get moving. The inspector's already out of sight."

Liz took out her map. "She said the store's called Luggage Unlimited. It's at the far end of the mall. Believe it or not, that's eight city blocks away."

Mrs. Austen smiled. "We should rent one of those electric carts for weary shoppers."

"Or hire one of the mall's rickshaws! What a way to arrive at the scene of the crime."

A small crowd had gathered at Luggage Unlimited outside the yellow police tapes that blocked the entrance. Escorted by Inspector Winter Eagle, the Austens entered the store. At first it appeared normal. Suitcases stood in careful displays, attaché cases were arranged to appeal to the business shopper, and soft leather purses had been hung in neat rows. But, further back in an upper display area, there was terrible damage. Purses were slashed, suitcases twisted and useless, and pictures had been torn from the walls and smashed underfoot. Tom and Liz saw an officer questioning a man and woman who wore the traditional clothes of India. Then they became aware of the graffiti spray-painted around the walls.

Paki, the savage words said. *Go home, Paki. We don't want your kind. Pakis out!!*

3

The next morning Tom and Liz were still upset as they had breakfast at one of the mall's restaurants. "Why are some people so cruel?" Liz said to her parents. "It's *terrible* to hurt others like that."

"Racists are afraid," Mrs. Austen said. "Afraid of change, afraid of strangers, afraid of anything that threatens their narrow world." She pushed a strand of hair out of her face. "After we get home I'll be in court on a hate-mail case. I don't think I've ever been so angry about anything since I became a lawyer. I just can't believe some people can be so ignorant."

"I just wish I could *do* something," Tom said. "It was horrible last night at the luggage store. I felt so helpless."

Mr. Austen squeezed the back of Tom's hand. "You

and Liz were great. When we were asking questions you really showed the Gills that you cared about them." He lifted a coffee cup to his lips. "Besides which . . . Ouch! That's hot."

Tom grinned. "Remember how I bugged Mom until she quit smoking? Now I'm going to work on you about drinking coffee. Your love affair with caffeine must stop!"

"He's right," Liz said. "Besides, that cream you put in your coffee turns to leather once it hits your stomach."

"Where's all this stuff come from?"

"Health class, of course. It's got the best videos in school."

Dietmar nodded. "She's right, Mr. Austen. Ever seen close-ups of lungs dripping tar? Every smoker in school was butting out at noon hour."

"It's hard to believe kids your age smoke," Mr. Austen said as he shook his head. "The world's gone haywire."

"Want some more bad news?" Liz spread some jam on a thick slice of toast and took a bite. "Mmmmm, that's good. Anyway, Dad, hang on to your cane. The next big fad may be tattoos."

"*What?*"

"You know, those weird designs on peoples' . . ."

"I know what a tattoo is, Liz. But you're telling me . . . ?"

"That kids are getting into tattoos. Isn't that right, Dietmar?"

"Maybe, but I haven't . . ."

"I don't believe it," Mr. Austen interrupted. "What'll the next fad be? Lobotomies?"

Mrs. Austen patted his cheek. "Remember your

blood pressure, dear. Now just drink your coffee and try to relax."

Tom glanced up at the skylight as a cloud drifted past, momentarily blocking the sunshine. They were surrounded by greenery, from plants in bamboo pots to ferns spikier than a rock star's hair, to the 14 trees he'd counted below. The restaurant was shaped like a horseshoe, with an open space at its centre; one floor down were the tables, fountains and trees of a fast-food arcade.

"I love this place," he said.

Liz nodded her agreement. "Dad, is there anything new on the bomb?"

"Nothing major, but the police figured out how the luggage store was broken into. They've recommended the owners install an intruder detector in the showroom—the Gills said they'd get one right away."

"How'd the break-in happen?"

"Apparently there's a vast open space above all the stores. It's a huge, dark crawlspace—there's barely room to stand up in it. Apparently street kids used to sneak around up there at night. They'd lift out ceiling tiles, drop into stores to steal things, then escape through the crawlspace. Security thought they'd solved that problem, but somebody must have found a new way into it. It looks like that person's responsible for the damage to Luggage Unlimited."

Mrs. Austen poured herself some water from a jug. "I understand the Gills found the mess when they opened the store in the afternoon. Why were they so late opening the store?"

"A family emergency at her sister's farm. They were both needed, so the store was closed for the morning."

"So," Tom said, "that racist creep knew it would be easy to break in." He looked at the waitress who was approaching with more coffee. "Did you hear what happened yesterday at Luggage Unlimited?"

"Yes, I did. It was disgraceful." She turned to Mrs. Austen. "I enjoy seeing you folks every morning. You'll be here for a while, won't you? I'll bet those security guards are really glad that you're here to help."

"You mean because of that bomb being discovered?" Mrs. Austen shook her head. "We're not leaving. My husband says there's no immediate danger, so that's good enough for me. That crazy person who left the bomb will be eating every meal behind bars soon."

"Let's hope so. I've been working here since the mall opened and I love it. Plus, my relatives are arriving from Hungary next week to see this place. I don't want anything to go wrong while they're here, but I guess I'm just overreacting."

"Hey," Tom said, "they've actually heard of this mall in Hungary?"

"Sure. People from all over the world—even Siberia—have sat in that booth."

"Fantastic." He took out his notebook. "What a great addition to my trivia about the mall." He made notes, then glanced at the others. "Here's another test: You know those chandeliers we've seen around? How many lights in each?" When no one could answer he said, "Two thousand. Next question: How many people work here?"

"That one's easy," the waitress said. "Fifteen thousand. But if lots of people hear about yesterday's trouble or if there are any more bombs, people might be afraid to work here. You've got to catch that bomber fast, Mr. Austen."

"You're right." He drank the rest of his coffee. "Which reminds me, I'm meeting Inspector Winter Eagle in 15 minutes at Bourbon Street."

"May we come, Dad?" Liz asked.

"Sorry, sweetheart. This meeting's only for senior police brass and officials from the city and provincial governments. There's lots of important people worried about the bomber."

Tom stood up. "Well, Dad, seeing that you've got everything under control, I'm going to try to find out who's hurting the Gills."

Mrs. Austen touched his hand. "Be careful."

"It's okay, Mom, I'll stay in the mall." He looked at his notebook. "Know how many security guards this place has?"

She nodded. "Fifty, but I say it again: be careful."

Tom kissed her cheek, then looked at Liz. "Want to come?"

"I can't. Yesterday I met someone really nice and told her I'd meet her this morning."

He turned to Dietmar. "How about you? Or will it be another morning in front of the soaps?"

"Nope, I'll come with you." Dietmar shovelled a leftover muffin into his mouth as he stood up. Then he pulled a paperback out of his hip pocket. "Here," he mumbled to Liz through the muffin, "I forgot to return it earlier. Sorry, I got food on page 56."

"Thanks a lot," Liz grumbled, flipping to the page. "I hope it's not . . ." For a second her eyes bulged; then a scream ripped through the restaurant when a black spider tumbled from the book into her lap. As people turned to stare, she leapt from the booth, slapping frantic hands at her clothes. "Where is it? Where is it?"

"Right here." Dietmar knelt to pick up the spider. Stroking its little plastic head he murmured, "Poor pet, all those nasty screams must be upsetting. Shall I take you home to the joke shop?"

Liz grabbed for the water jug but was restrained by her mother. "Take it easy, sweetheart. Do any damage and his parents could sue." Then she looked at Dietmar. "Relax with the gags, okay, or I may have to lean on you."

"Sure thing, Mrs. Austen."

Grinning, Dietmar left the restaurant. Tom gave his sister an apologetic shrug, then hurried out of the restaurant after a brief, hungry stare at the display of Black Forest cakes and *gâteaux au chocolat* being prepared for lunch. Together with Dietmar he descended an escalator to the indoor sea, where brilliant sunshine streamed down onto the white sails of the *Santa Maria*.

"See those cannons?" Tom pointed at the deck. "You'll want to know they're fakes."

"Why should I want to know that, Austen?"

"To impress everyone back home with your knowledge of the supermall. Otherwise you'll be telling them that it's shaped like a TV screen."

"I've seen lots of things."

"Sure! The Drop of Doom, the Mindbender and the Sky Screamer."

"That's enough."

"Our walkabout this morning will do you good. With me as your guide you'll see amazing sights. Besides, maybe we'll hear something about the attack—

there are hundreds of kids around this mall. Someone must have heard rumours."

"This reminds me, and not happily I might add, of our little excursion to Blood Alley Square in Vancouver. I hope this isn't going to be a repeat."

"Not a chance." Tom moved along the railing to get a better view of the dolphin pool on the far side of the sea. "Compared to this mission, Blood Alley Square was a picnic."

"Then forget it."

Tom grabbed his arm. "Come back here! I'll protect you."

Dietmar laughed. "Only until we meet a pitbull terrier. Remember walking to school last winter when that one came charging at us across his yard?"

"I didn't think he was chained."

"You sure went up that tree in a hurry."

Over at the dolphin pool a trainer appeared through a door in the rocky wall that overlooked a small beach and the water. The excited faces of the dolphins immediately appeared from underwater, squealing for treats from the pail the man had just set down. As he made hand signals the dolphins disappeared under the surface, then leapt together from the water. For one splendid moment they glistened in midair, then plunged back beneath the waves. A moment later they were back to receive their reward, and the man continued to toss fish into the dolphins' mouths as he coaxed them to slide further up on the beach. Finally, when they had slipped back into the pool, Tom and Dietmar continued walking.

"I'd like that job," Dietmar said. "Dolphins are great."

Inside a video arcade coloured lights flashed like alien eyes and the haunted mechanical voices of the games called out challenges. They watched a boy wearing glasses play for a while, then Tom asked if he could join in.

"You're going against Manitoba's finest," he warned. "Want to risk it?"

"This arcade's my summer home," the boy said. His teeth were thick with braces. "This game is my girlfriend."

"Too bad about the luggage store," Tom said as images whirled on the screen and his hands moved nimbly. "I guess you heard?"

"Sure."

"How do you feel about what happened?"

The boy shrugged. "Not good, but what can you do?"

"Any idea who did it?"

"The Skull. Everyone knows that."

"Who?"

"There's a guy around this mall who calls himself the Skull. He's got a shaved head and the brainpower of a slug. Steer clear of him—he's real mean and his hero's Adolf Hitler. Get the picture?"

"Sure." Tom looked in amazement at his score. "Wow, Oban, do you see that? A *Guinness Book of Records* qualifier."

"It's beatable," Dietmar said with a shrug.

The boy wearing the glasses nodded. "Your friend's right. Watch my moves."

Minutes later Tom and Dietmar walked out of the arcade, stunned by the score achieved so easily by the boy. From somewhere in the mall came the sound of music, booming down the corridor and making shop windows vibrate. They hurried toward it and joined a crowd outside a huge bookstore. On a raised platform a band was performing, fronted by a teenage boy in T-shirt and jeans. One hand on his guitar, one on the microphone, his eyes were closed and sweat poured down his face as he sang about losing at love.

"It's the Rock the Mall contest!" Tom moved closer. "This must be Creatures of the Night. I heard they're a great band and it's true!"

"What's the Rock the Mall contest?" Dietmar asked. "Nobody told me about it."

"The hottest new talent in the West is in this contest. There are musicians competing all over the mall this week. The winner gets a video contract, plus a trip to Hamilton for the national finals."

"Why weren't we invited?"

"Because our band belongs in a garage, which is why we only play there. If you came to more rehearsals maybe we'd get somewhere."

"Then don't rehearse Saturday mornings. I'm still asleep."

They stayed for the entire show, then reluctantly moved on as it ended. "*I wanna be a star*," Dietmar exclaimed. "I wanna be on the cover of *Rolling Stone*." With his hands playing an imaginary guitar, he side-danced along the corridor while shoppers stared and shook their heads. A little girl holding a balloon watched gravely, thumb in mouth, then presented the balloon to Dietmar.

"Thanks, kid!" He grinned at Tom. "She knows true talent."

"Hey!" Tom shouted at Dietmar as he started walking away. "Give her back the balloon!"

Not far away another crowd had gathered beside a bamboo cage, where two tiger cubs rolled together in a mock battle. For a moment they paused, gazing at the people with enormous and gentle eyes, then returned to their game.

"I feel sorry for them," Dietmar said. "Stuck in a cage."

"The mall owns a game farm. The animals spend a lot of time out there."

"Okay folks," a woman said from beside a camera. "Who wants a picture taken with a tiger on your lap?"

"She must be crazy," Dietmar said. "Who'd spend money on that?"

"I would."

Taking out his wallet, Tom stared at the thin collection of bills. "Where'd it all go?"

"Remember those five trips on the Mindbender yesterday? They didn't come cheap."

"Sure, but . . ." Tom counted his money. "Are there pickpockets around?"

"The defective detective," Dietmar snorted. "Since when do pickpockets only take some of your cash?"

Tom shrugged. "I guess you're right. I've been spending too much." Taking out a bill, he paid the woman for a picture and sat down. Her assistant opened the cage and lifted out a cub. "They've just had a bath, so they're a bit crabby."

"I don't care, I love cats!" The cub was on his lap just long enough for Tom to stroke the soft fur, then the shutter clicked and the tiger was returned to its cage. When the picture was ready Tom studied the cub's face before putting it safely away.

"What a great souvenir!"

"Keep spending your money like that, Austen, and there'll be nothing left for gifts. By the way, what're you taking home for me?"

"Why would I do that?"

Dietmar shrugged. "It seems the thoughtful thing to do."

"I got Mr. Stones the perfect gift yesterday. A key chain with the logo of his import. Have you seen the store that sells nothing but car accessories?"

Dietmar shook his head. "I'm getting hungry."

"You just had breakfast."

"So what? I just heard my stomach complain. Let's get something at the Ice Palace."

"Okay, but I want to learn more about this guy who calls himself the Skull."

They reached the Ice Palace a few minutes later. The size of a regulation NHL rink, it sparkled under the sunshine that poured down from high-domed skylights. "Those windows are computer controlled," Tom said. "Somehow they keep the temperature constant in here." Stores on two levels surrounded the rink, and a lot of people were standing at the railings, watching the skaters.

"The Oilers practise here. During the summer sometimes they even have exhibition games between a few Oilers and guys from other teams. There's one this Friday night, but I doubt you're interested."

"Not when I can watch *Wall Street Week*."

"That money programme? What's so interesting about it?"

"Pretty soon I'll be investing in stocks and bonds. I

want to know which ones make megabucks."

"You're probably right. So what do you recommend?"

"That we get some food."

At a nearby stand they bought Coney Island hot dogs, and sat down at a table by the rink. Munching silently, Tom and Dietmar stared at figure skaters swirling past, wearing fancy costumes. When they'd finished eating, Tom turned to a boy about his age who was sitting at the next table.

"You ever heard of a guy who calls himself the Skull?"

The boy shook his head, but the question got a reaction from a couple of older boys who were sitting nearby with their feet up on a railing, hands in the pockets of their leather jackets, and boredom on their faces. Hearing Tom's question they turned to stare at him, then at Dietmar, then at each other.

"Hey you," one of them said to Tom. "Come here."

4

Tom hesitated, then walked over. "Yeah?"

"How come you're asking about the Skull?"

Tom looked at the boy's hostile eyes. "You know him?"

"Maybe. Why's it important?"

"Where can I find the Skull?"

"He's around." The boy flicked his cigarette onto the ice. "Why?"

"I'm just curious." Turning, Tom walked away. "Come on," he said to Dietmar, "let's get moving."

"Gladly!"

As they left the Ice Palace Tom glanced at a store window. Reflected in the glass were the two Neanderthals, following close behind. "Interesting guys."

"I'll say! Now we're in trouble, thanks to you asking questions."

"We're perfectly safe. This mall's got lots of security guards walking around in disguise and besides, we've struck pay dirt. Those two losers actually know the Skull."

"Sure, and they're following us. What possible use is that?"

"I don't know. Maybe they'll meet the Skull and we'll get a look at him."

"This is turning into a real fun morning, Austen."

"It could be worse. What if the soaps were all reruns?"

"Where are we going now?"

"Luggage Unlimited. I want to tell the Gills what we've learned."

On the way to the store they paused to watch another band performing near a group of fountains that gushed upwards from a marble pool, the water lit by orange and blue and red spotlights. "There's 43 individual fountains," Dietmar said, after counting them. "Put that on your list." He watched Tom make a note, then added, "That'll cost you, by the way. I don't research trivia for free."

"Forget it!"

"I'll expect a cheque by tomorrow, at the latest."

A few minutes later they entered Luggage Unlimited, where a boy their age stood behind the counter. His smile was friendly. "Hi," he said. "My name's Neil Raj Gill. Need help finding something?"

"Not exactly." Tom introduced himself and Dietmar, then explained he'd been at the store the evening before. "You weren't here, but I met your parents. I've got some information they might want."

"My mom's working today. I'll get her."

Mrs. Gill came from the office with a puzzled frown. "You've learned something?"

"It's nothing definite," Tom replied, "but someone called the Skull is probably the person who broke in here last night."

Neil Raj nodded. "I've had some trouble with him before."

"I'll phone the police," Mrs. Gill said. "Can you give them proof, Tom?"

"No, Ma'am. Just rumours."

"I'll tell them anyway."

As she placed the call Neil Raj looked out the window. The two punks were watching the store, hands in the pockets of their leather jackets and scowls on their mean faces. "Those two hang out with the Skull. I've seen them all together."

"They've been following us," Dietmar said. "It's giving me the creeps."

"Me too." Tom looked at Neil Raj. "I wouldn't mind losing them. This store's got a back door, right?"

"You bet. Follow me."

As they walked through the store Tom noticed that all signs of damage had been removed. The suitcases stood in neat rows, the walls had been freshly painted and there were new pictures. "It must have taken all night to fix things so quickly," he said. "Are you worried it'll happen again?"

"That's not likely." Neil Raj paused in the upper display area to point at a tiny red light flashing from a small plastic device on the ceiling. "That's our new intruder detector. If anyone moves in here at night, *zap*. A siren starts wailing and a message flashes to security headquarters and the police. The guards can have this place completely blocked off within two minutes."

"That's still 120 seconds," Tom said. "Enough time for him to escape."

"Maybe so, but at least the store won't be trashed."

Mrs. Gill joined them. "The police thanked me for the information, but they need some kind of real proof." She smiled at Tom. "You're very kind to help."

"I wish I could do more."

Neil Raj looked at his mother. "Okay to take an hour off? Heather's singing in the contest and I want to be there, cheering." After she'd given her permission he turned to Tom and Dietmar. "Want to come? I'd like you to meet Heather."

"She's your girlfriend?" Dietmar asked.

"No, she's 18. I play streetball with her brother, so she's kind of a friend."

They entered a storage area at the back of the store. Cartons were piled on shelves that reached to the ceiling, brooms and a vacuum cleaner stood in one corner, and cool air blew from a vent in the wall.

"I just thought of something," Tom said. "The police figure the intruder dropped down from the ceiling, but maybe he came through that air conditioning vent."

Neil Raj pointed up at a ceiling tile. "See those scuffs and scratches? Those were fresh last night, and the air conditioning grill didn't show any sign of damage."

"You're right. So much for my theory."

They entered a long corridor where nothing could be seen but the back doors of other stores. "This leads to another part of the mall," Neil Raj said. "It's a perfect route to slip away from those gorillas who were following you."

Tom looked up at the big aluminum shaft that carried air conditioning to the stores. "I'm still suspicious about those ducts. They're big enough to crawl through and they must go everywhere in the mall. It's the ideal secret route."

Dietmar smiled at Neil Raj. "I've listened to this stuff for years, ever since he discovered Frank and Joe Hardy. Now he reads le Carré, but it's still the same old story—hidden clues and villains crawling through air conditioning ducts. Tell me about it!"

Neil Raj laughed. "I'm surprised you two are friends. You're totally different from each other."

At the end of the corridor they stepped through a doorway back into the mall. Tom breathed a sigh of relief as he was once again surrounded by people. "I guess I was more nervous than I thought. Hey, what's that gizmo? I haven't seen it before."

A two-storey device nearby was producing a cacophony of sounds: *BONG! BONG!* and *BLAM—BLAM—BLAM* and *TING! TING!* A crowd had gathered around to watch billiard balls follow a twisting route down, twirling around and around in long spirals, triggering hammers that struck against gongs, striking brass cymbals, and performing other noisy tricks before being lifted to the heights to begin the journey anew.

"Bizarre," Dietmar laughed. "What strange genius created that thing?" He looked at his watch. "Say, how about a quick trip on the Mindbender? Have we got time before your friend sings?"

"Sure, let's go for it."

After a quick walk they passed through the arched entrance to Galaxyland, the indoor amusement park. Music played loudly, people jammed the sidewalks and a giant swing swirled above, but the scene was dominated by the Mindbender. Fourteen stories high, the roller coaster's triple loops were coiled like a sea serpent, and rose so far above them that the tops were barely visible under the sloped roof.

"Let's get moving!" As Tom ran toward the ticket booth he watched a car drop straight down with everyone inside screaming. "I can't wait! This thing is amazing!"

Minutes later they were in a car and he was rapidly changing his mind. "I can't do it," he moaned as it began moving. "I want out."

"You say that every time, Austen. Besides, it's too late," Dietmar yelled. "Here we go!"

The car rapidly climbed straight up toward the roof. People were screaming by the time they reached the top; Tom's knuckles were white on the safety rail. Then the car fell. Straight down, a terrifying drop into emptiness, the wind loud in his ears; then the car abruptly reached bottom and roared up inside a loop. Over they went, upside down, and flew to the heights again, before falling once more. Everyone on the ride was yelling and screaming with excitement.

With an ear-splitting screech of brakes, the ride finally ended. Everyone staggered out, shaking their heads in disbelief. Neil Raj stood on one leg and pounded the side of his head. "I feel like I've got water on the brain."

"You're out of focus," Tom said. "So's everyone else."

"Come on," Dietmar yelled. "The Drop of Doom's next."

"Not until my stomach feels normal."

"I'll stay with Tom," Neil Raj said. "We'll go play some games."

"Okay. I'll meet you guys there."

They were both good at Speed Shifters and equally useless at Championship Darts and Vegas Prize Ring. Then someone approached. He was a bit older than they were, with mean eyes and a totally shaved head. Beside his mouth was a long, ragged scar.

The Skull.

Just behind him stood the gorillas in leather jackets. "Yeah?" he said to Tom. "You're looking for me?"

Tom swallowed. "Uh . . . yes."

"So?"

"I'm . . . well, you . . . someone said you knew something. About what happened last night." Tom paused, but the Skull didn't speak. "You know, at the luggage store."

At that moment Dietmar appeared at Tom's side. "What's going on, Austen?"

"Just a little trouble."

The Skull looked at Neil Raj, then spat on the ground. "*Pakis.*"

"Hey," Tom said. "That's pretty . . ."

Neil Raj moved between Tom and the Skull. His hands were clenched into hard fists, but his voice was calm as he said, "Listen you. About that word *Paki*. It's ugly and it's ignorant. Besides, my family came from India, not Pakistan, and I was born in Vancouver."

Silence.

"Did you trash my parents' store?"

"Get lost."

"I'm sure it was you. Leave our store alone."

"You're giving me orders, Paki?" The Skull signalled to his friends, who moved closer. "That's not such a good idea."

Dietmar looked at Neil Raj. "Come on, let's get out of here."

"In a minute."

A man in a golf shirt and slacks approached the group. "Good day, gentlemen." He showed them a photo ID card. "I'm a security guard. What's going on? Things look a little tense here." When nobody spoke he pointed to the nearest exit. "Why don't you all move along?"

The Skull gave Neil Raj a dirty look, then walked away with his friends. As Tom and the others left by a different exit, Dietmar released a sigh.

"Wow! That was tense."

Tom looked at Neil Raj. "Do you think there's a link between the bomb found at the Café Orleans and the break-in at your store?"

"No. I'm pretty sure the Skull trashed our store, but he's not bright enough to get his hands on a bomb. Besides, what's his motive? I think the bomber must be someone with a grudge against the mall or something like that. And you've got to have brains to figure out how to make a bomb, and get it in here without being seen."

A series of ponds divided the corridor they were following. Coins gleamed underwater, fountains gurgled and palm trees reached to the skylights above. At the Ice Palace they rode up in a glass-walled elevator while watching the skaters make swirling patterns on the ice.

Stepping out of the cage they saw a crowd gathered around a platform. A golden-haired girl had just finished a song and the audience was yelling its appreciation. The girl grinned, her big eyes shining.

"She's really cute!" Dietmar said.

Tom looked at Neil Raj. "You actually know her?"

He shrugged, grinning. "Yup."

Heather's band wore stetsons and red satin outfits; she was in a white skirt and shimmering silver blouse. Picking up her guitar, she started a country song that had the people stomping their feet and clapping their hands.

"She gets my vote," Tom yelled as the song ended and everyone cheered.

Liz appeared out of the crowd, smiling. "Isn't Heather great? She's the girl I met yesterday."

After Liz was introduced to Neil Raj they listened to a final song. Heather took a bow, then came down off the stage to sign autographs and talk excitedly to the people who surrounded her. Finally Neil Raj brought her over to meet Tom and Dietmar. Her blue-green eyes were very large and beautiful.

"Great show," Tom said. "Congratulations."

"Thanks! Could you imagine if my band actually won the contest?"

"You'll do it," Dietmar said. "How about an autograph?" He borrowed Tom's notebook, ripped out a page and handed it to Heather. "Please include the year."

"Sure, but why?"

"It makes the autograph more valuable. Some day that scrap of paper will finance my first BMW."

"What a lovely thought!" Heather turned to Neil Raj. "I'm sorry about the store. I'll phone your Mom and Dad today to see how they're doing."

"Thanks, Heather. Maybe . . ."

He was interrupted by the arrival of a worried man in a rumpled suit. "Heather," he said, "there's a photographer here from the *Journal*. Can you pose for her?"

"Sure." She looked at the others. "This is Mr. Sutton. He's my manager."

"Hi there." He gave them a brief nod, then turned to Heather. "Come on, kid. We need the publicity. Save the socializing for later."

As they walked away Dietmar looked at his watch. "Hey, I'm outta here. It's almost noon and I'm not in front of the tube. Today Samantha and Robert find out about her uncle's fortune from the lawyer. I can't miss the show."

After Neil Raj made plans to go watersliding with Tom, he left for the store. Liz was leaning over a railing watching the figure skaters when Tom turned and smiled at her. "So what's the secret?"

"Huh?"

"You're excited about something. I can tell."

"You're right! I've got a date for Friday. His name's Chad. Heather introduced me."

"Where are you going?"

"To Galaxyland."

"What's this guy like?"

"Don't worry, I'll be okay."

"Want me and Dietmar to come along as chaperones?"

"*No!!*"

Laughing, Tom suggested they look at the piranhas. They walked along beside the curved upper railing to a large aquarium where the deadly fish swam among green ferns. Tom leaned close to the glass feeling brave as the tough little faces gazed back at him. "They don't scare me."

"Read that sign," Liz said. "*Feeding frenzies occur when blood is drawn.*"

"Now they scare me."

"This glass reflects well. I just saw someone take our picture."

Turning, Tom saw a man wearing glasses walk away. Attached to his belt was a leather pouch. "Is that a holster?"

Liz shook her head. "He put his camera in it." She looked at Tom. "Feel like following him? He was watching us earlier and making notes. And I'm sure I've seen him before."

"Okay, let's . . ."

Tom paused, looking puzzled. The music had suddenly stopped and all the speakers around the rink were silent. Then a voice urgently announced, "*Code Red, Code Red.*"

5

After a brief pause the announcement was repeated, but this time with a store's name included: *Code Red, Full Fathom Down.* "That place isn't far," Liz said, quickly consulting her map. "Let's get moving!"

People stared as they raced through the mall, unaware that the secret warning of a maximum alert was the cause of their mad dash to Full Fathom Down. Arriving there at the same moment as the security guards, Tom and Liz were surprised to see Inspector Winter Eagle already inside the store.

"We've got another bomb," she said. "Your dad's dealing with it."

"Should we leave?" Tom asked as security guards began clearing the area.

The inspector shook her head. "Naturally we don't

want shoppers around, but your dad says this bomb isn't set to explode either."

"Was a wire left disconnected, like the first one?"

She nodded. "More bad news for the mall, but at least no one's been hurt yet."

"How did you and Dad get here so fast?"

"We were questioning people at stores in this corridor when we heard shouts." She glanced at a man slumped in a chair at the back of the store. He was about 30, with a fleshy nose and thin brown hair. Shock had drained his face of colour. "That's Benn Dunn, a sales assistant here. He discovered the bomb and ran out of the store, yelling at people to clear the area."

On display around the walls were face masks, flippers, oxygen tanks and other gear for scuba lovers. A poster showed divers plunging from a yacht into the aqua waters of a tropical paradise, while another pictured some people on a dock at the mall's own indoor sea. Tom and Liz walked through the store with the Inspector as she explained, "Benn Dunn found the bomb in the storage area at the back. It was either planted there overnight or some time after the store opened this morning."

"Wouldn't he have seen it carried into the store?"

"Not if it was hidden inside something."

In the cluttered storage room cool air blew through a vent in the wall, and big shelves were filled with cartons and scuba equipment. Mr. Austen stood near the tiny washroom, where a package was visible under the sink. "The red wire tells the story," he said. "The explosives are connected to that alarm clock, which was rigged to detonate them at exactly noon. But again this time the red wire was deliberately not attached. The bomb couldn't have exploded."

"The bomber didn't forget to do it?" Tom asked.

"Not a chance. This person is an expert."

Tom looked at the area set aside for staff to relax; sitting in a chair was a handsome man in his early 30s, with a good tan and hair bleached blond by the sun.

"My name's Christopher Dixon," he said. "I'm the manager of Full Fathom Down. Your dad's been telling me about your exploits in the past. I hope you're going to help too."

"Thanks, Mr. Dixon. We . . ."

"Please, call me Christopher."

"Do you have any idea how the bomb got into your store?"

"The back door's a possibility. It connects to a service corridor where deliveries are made, but it was locked all yesterday and this morning."

Tom glanced at his sister and saw that her eyes had glazed over as she stared at the man. Shaking his head, he asked, "What about the ceiling tiles? Could the bomber have dropped into the store that way?"

Before Christopher could answer a woman appeared in the doorway. She was about 24 years old; the dramatic black of her hair was matched by the colour of her eyes and the silk dress she wore. Gold jewellery shone on her fingers, and at her neck and ears. She extended a hand to Inspector Winter Eagle. "I'm Carroll McAndrews, owner of this store." Turning to Christopher the woman said, "You're okay?"

"Sure, I'm fine. But trouble like this isn't going to do the mall any good. What'll we all do if people stop shopping here?"

"Father won't let this situation continue—he'll make sure the mystery is solved." Carroll looked at Inspector Winter Eagle. "My father has several stores in this mall."

"I know. It was the talk of Edmonton about how much money he paid to set up and furnish the stores."

"It wasn't his money."

"What do you mean?"

Carroll hesitated, then shrugged. "Well, I guess it's no secret. A couple of years ago Father was in San Diego on holiday and happened to meet a wealthy woman who lived there. Apparently she was involved with some local, but the guy was poor as a church mouse. He couldn't match Father's gifts of long-stemmed roses and jewellery. Before long she dumped the local, and suddenly I had a stepmother."

"She married your father?"

"That's right." Carroll shrugged. "But I hardly know the woman. We only met once, at the wedding in California. She's terrified of flying, so she's never been to Edmonton. Father visits her whenever possible, but in my opinion it's not much of a marriage."

"Your father used her money to set up stores in the mall?"

"Correct. It was always his big dream to be part of the supermall." She glanced around at the scuba gear. "Then he arranged this store for me. I guess it was supposed to make me happy."

Mr. Austen looked at her. "Edmonton seems an odd location for this kind of place."

"Not really. Our scuba club dives in the indoor sea every morning before the mall opens for business. Plus there's oil money in Alberta, so wealthy locals holiday in the world's scuba capitals with equipment purchased from my store." She looked at Christopher. "This man's the reason why my store's so successful. He knows the sport inside out."

Inspector Winter Eagle looked at him. "How long have you worked here?"

"Since Carroll opened the store, about four months ago. I came to Edmonton to dive the indoor sea and decided to stay. I got a job guiding visitors around the mall, then met Carroll and she asked me to be manager of her store." He looked at the Inspector. "I'm really angry about the bomber. I'd like to find the person who's responsible."

"Don't take the law into your own hands, Mr. Dixon." Inspector Winter Eagle looked at the notes she'd been making. "What about Benn Dunn? What's his story?"

"He's only been here about a month," Carroll replied. "He appeared out of nowhere, some kind of a drifter, but he's a great diver. The customers really respect his advice."

"I've got an idea," Tom said to Carroll. "Maybe the bomber's motive is to get revenge against your dad. If his stores suffer financially maybe he'd be ruined."

"Nope. My stepmother has lots more money in the bank. Besides, why would someone want to hurt my father?"

"I'm not sure. Maybe . . ."

Tom was interrupted by the arrival of a huge man in the doorway. He stared at his thick white hair, fierce eyes under bushy brows and bronze skin that had been seared by a lifetime of sun and wind. Towering above them all, he wore an expensive cowboy hat and a three-piece suit perfectly tailored to his body.

Inspector Winter Eagle broke the silence. "This is Carroll's father, Danniel McAndrews."

Mr. McAndrews scratched a match on the sole of his cowboy boot to light a cigar. After briefly inspecting the bomb he asked for details of the investigation and then, as smoke stung the others' eyes, he said, "Last year nine million people visited this mall. Lots of people already know about yesterday's scare, and more are going to hear about today's discovery. You know how easily people panic. Find that bomber fast, Inspector, or we'll be lucky to have nine visitors next year." He turned to Carroll. "Hang out some sale signs. Business will take a real nose-dive now, unless we do something."

"I'll make my own decision about a sale, Father. It's my store, remember?"

"This place was set up with my money and became a success because of my expert advice."

"Then why don't you run it, too? I can go back to diving in the Caribbean. I hate what owning a bunch of stores has done to you, Father. You're trying to build an empire and it's the only thing you care about."

When the big man didn't reply she sighed. Then she looked at Tom and Liz. "Ever tried scuba?"

Liz nodded. "Yes, we've both got our certificates. Any chance of diving with your club?"

"Maybe." She picked up a speargun from a shelf. "I was wondering if you'd be in the market for some good equipment like this. I'll give you a special discount."

Liz shivered. "We took lessons on using a speargun, but I hate them."

"Too bad." Carroll pretended to take aim at a carton. "I love these things." Putting down the speargun, she walked into the display area and the others followed. More police officers had arrived and one was questioning Benn Dunn, who was staring at the floor with sullen eyes.

Seeing Inspector Winter Eagle the officer said, "This man won't cooperate."

"Why should I?" Benn Dunn muttered. "I haven't broken any laws."

Christopher stepped forward. "A crime's been committed right here in our store. I want you to help these officers."

Benn Dunn flashed him a look of intense dislike. "I have to take your orders all day, but not this time."

A red glow spread under Christopher's tan. "You've got to help them."

"I told them the facts once. I don't have to answer the same questions again."

Tom glanced sympathetically at Christopher, then turned toward the front door, where a woman of about 20 was trying to get past a security guard. "My boyfriend's in here! He could have been killed!" With surprising strength for her size she pushed aside the guard and ran to hug Christopher. "Oh, Chris," she sobbed, her cheeks glistening with tears. "I was so worried! I heard the news on the car radio when I was driving to work. I almost drove off the Whitemud."

Gently freeing himself, Christopher smiled down at her. "I'm sorry you were scared." Turning to the others, he said, "This is my friend, Lisa deVita. She's one of the mall's dolphin trainers."

Carroll had been watching the other woman through narrowed eyes. Now she said, "Late for work again, Ms. deVita? I'm surprised my father doesn't have you fired."

Mr. McAndrews shook his head. "Not when we've got such a great dolphin show. But my daughter's got a point, Lisa. Why are you late for work?"

"I slept in."

Carroll shook her head. "Why's it so difficult to get reliable employees these days? If I . . ."

"Listen lady," Lisa interrupted angrily. "One more remark like that and you'll regret it!" Letting go of Christopher she walked to the door and turned to stare at Carroll. "Another thing: you keep your claws off my man or *you'll be sorry.*"

As Lisa stormed away Liz followed. Tom stayed in the store a few minutes more, then went into the mall to find his sister. When he did, she was smiling.

"Guess what, brother?"

"Major information?"

"Nope. A chance to see backstage at the dolphin show. Lisa deVita's one of the trainers and I just got permission for a special tour. Not only that, she's part of the scuba club and she's invited us to dive tomorrow morning. The club's got equipment we can use."

"Terrific! Say, what's with Lisa and Carroll? Are they both in love with Christopher?"

"It looks that way. They don't exactly get along, do they?"

"I'll say. Sparks must fly whenever they meet."

* * *

At exactly seven the next morning Tom and Liz stood on a small dock. Soft sunlight from far above touched the sails of the *Santa Maria* and made the blue water look cool and inviting. As Lisa deVita prepared the equipment and chatted to other club members, Liz studied the coral and make-believe crabs beneath the surface. "Whoever designed this mall should get a trophy. Everything looks so real! I love those statues and the pottery. Do you think Atlantis ever existed?"

"If it did, I feel sorry for the people when it sank," Lisa replied. "But the people around here don't seem to be having much luck either. I hope they find the bomber fast."

"I wonder if Carroll's father is upset?"

"Probably not. He's pretty self-confident." Lisa glanced at her watch. "Mr. McAndrews and Carroll will arrive at 7:15 A.M., on the dot. He's the world's most organized person and she's totally under his thumb."

The pair did arrive exactly on time. After brief words of greeting, father and daughter prepared in silence and plunged beneath the surface. Then Benn Dunn appeared, along with Christopher, who hugged Lisa and brushed her forehead with a kiss. "I've been doing a little investigating. I may even find the bomber before the police do."

"Oh, Chris, be careful! I can't bear the thought of anything happening."

After Christopher and Benn Dunn had dropped into the sea Liz stared across the water. "The sharks are hungry this morning. I can sense it."

Lisa smiled. "Want to cancel your dive?"

"Not a chance."

Tom and Liz waited for Lisa's thumbs-up signal. Then they tumbled into the water to enter a silent paradise where green plants swayed beside starfish clinging to jagged rocks. Tom motioned to Liz, pointing at a porcelain vase lying among the rocks; not far away were the statues of enormous temple dogs, their eyes staring forever at the waters that covered the lost treasures of Atlantis. Slowly Tom and Liz swam among the ruins, then turned to explore a treasure chest lying on the sandy bottom. They swam past gently moving strands of seaweed and pieces of jagged coral, then Tom almost choked with horror.

A shark was coming straight at him, ready to strike.

Desperately, Tom lifted his hands in a hopeless attempt to protect himself. But when the shark reached the glass wall of its tank it veered away, its body so close that every mark on the dark hide was visible. Turning, Tom saw that his sister's eyes were huge inside her mask. Motioning, she led them away from the sharks toward the *Santa Maria*. Through a glass wall they stared at a big grouper and other fish in the tank, then they swam to its stern where a realistic model captured a long-forgotten battle between a powerful sea-snake and some kind of aquatic dinosaur.

Then, as Tom and Liz began swimming toward the ribs of a sunken wreck, a figure in scuba gear appeared from its shadows and rose rapidly toward the surface, trailing a swarm of bubbles.

6

Reaching the surface, Tom and Liz tore off their masks. "That diver's in trouble," Tom yelled. "Where is he?"

"Over there, swimming toward the submarine dock. He looks okay now."

"It's Christopher! I wonder what happened?"

Within seconds Tom and Liz were with him. As other divers reached the dock Christopher showed them the wreckage of his air hose. "It was deliberately slashed! I could have drowned."

"What happened?"

Christopher glanced at Benn Dunn, who stood on the dock with sullen eyes. "We did the sub tunnel, then I signalled Benn that I wanted to explore the undersea wreck. There isn't enough room in there for two divers, so I swam into the wreck alone. I'd just entered some deep shadows when my air hose was slashed."

"But how?"

"I'm not sure—it happened so fast. I saw a hand and a piece of coral, then bubbles erupted around my mask."

"The attacker used a piece of coral to cut the hose?"

"I think so. No one in the club wears a knife."

A short time later, Lisa surfaced. When she heard the news there was an astonished silence, followed by an intense hug for Christopher.

"Get out of Edmonton, please! Take a holiday, I'll pay for it, just *escape*. Please!"

He laughed. "You think I'm a wimp? Come on, Lisa, drop the subject. I can take care of myself."

Soon after, Carroll and her father emerged from the water and were quickly told what had happened. Mr. McAndrews was furious at the latest bad news and left the area in a hurry. When he had gone, Carroll turned to the other divers.

"I'm sure it's one of you who's causing all this trouble," she said. "But whatever your scheme is, it won't work. I promise you: *It won't work*."

* * *

Tom was still talking about the air hose when he and Neil Raj reached the World Waterpark and bought tickets. "Who could have done it?"

Neil Raj watched a security guard check inside their sports bags, then wave them inside. "I don't know," he said as they entered the big locker room. "You said the sea was full of divers. They all had the opportunity."

"Sure, but they aren't the only possibility. What if some unknown person snuck into the mall early this morning when it was deserted? It would only take a couple of minutes to get into scuba gear and then hide underwater in the wreck."

"That's true, but why?"

"That's what I'm going to find out."

The air inside the waterpark was humid. Palm trees grew all over and they could hear the distant sound of waves rolling ashore on the artificial beach. Kids swirled down inside the translucent skins of the many enclosed waterslides and others were on a tree-lined volleyball court nearby. One of the teenagers watching them had a familiar face.

"Oh no," Tom said, "there's the Skull. And he just saw us."

"So what?" Neil Raj grinned as a loud horn blasted in the distance. "Hey, surf's up! Come on!"

Racing to the beach they plunged into the heart of a breaker and came up spluttering and laughing, then swam into the surf being created by a wave machine hidden under a waterfall at the pool's deep end. They body-surfed for a while, then headed for the beach. As they did, Tom saw the Skull and his two friends waiting for them.

"We've got company."

"Ignore them," Neil Raj replied as they waded ashore.

"Okay, but it won't be easy."

Grabbing their towels, they walked to a pair of empty beach chairs under a palm tree and sat down. The ugly trio followed to stand above them. Their chests were pasty white, but muscular.

"So!" The Skull stared at Neil Raj. "My first day here in months and you decide to spoil the view. So why don't you get out of here before I completely re-arrange your face?"

Tom looked across the water at a lifeguard standing on a platform. He was close enough to hear a yell for help, if he was needed.

"Why don't you guys leave us alone?" Tom said.

The Skull turned his cold eyes to him. "Shut your mouth. I don't like cops and I don't like their kids."

"How'd you know . . ."

Neil Raj raised a warning hand. "Ignore these guys. They'll go away before too long." He settled himself more comfortably on the chair. "Isn't that roof an amazing sight? Those arches are huge."

The Skull stepped closer. "Get out of here, Paki."

Neil Raj looked at him with steady eyes. "Not . . . a . . . chance," he said slowly. "Get the message?"

The Skull put his foot on the side of the chair and shoved it over. Neil Raj sprawled to the ground, then stood up rubbing his elbow. "You're pathetic," he said to the Skull. "Come on, Tom, let's go try the slides."

The others didn't follow, but they yelled a couple of insults as Neil Raj and Tom went to the stairs and began climbing. "Jerks," Neil Raj muttered.

"It was great how you handled the Skull. He was doing everything he could to get you mad."

"I know, but fights don't solve anything, and I'd never give that guy the satisfaction."

"I've been learning karate," Tom said, "but those guys still freak me."

"Me too," Neil Raj agreed.

At the top of the Blue Bullet slide Neil Raj sat down and waited for the go signal. "*Geronimo*," he yelled, disappearing down the tube. Tom waited for his green light and then let go, falling swiftly down, with the cascading water roaring in his ears. Then he was swallowed by a tunnel where he fell much faster; tiny blue lights above his head blurred together as he twisted down and down before falling through daylight into the pool where Neil Raj was waiting.

"Good times!" Tom yelled.

Then he saw the Skull and his friends. They were leaving the waterpark, but Tom was sure they'd meet again.

* * *

More than 50 mirrors surrounded Heather and Liz as they took an escalator to the mall's upper level. "Did you hear about the scuba diver?" Liz asked.

"Sure. Actually, I know Christopher."

"Really? How's that?"

"I was in his scuba store once and he was flirting with me." Heather smiled. "I told him to try someone his own age."

"Did he get angry?"

"No, he just laughed. Then we started talking. Since then we've often met for coffee. He's really interested in my career. He thinks I can be a megastar." She smiled shyly. "That's my dream, but Mr. Sutton doesn't agree."

"Who's Mr. Sutton?"

"My manager. You met him yesterday."

"Oh. Yeah."

"Mr. Sutton's always talking about one step at a time. He didn't want me to enter the Rock the Mall contest."

"But why?"

"He doesn't want me recording yet. In his opinion I need another year of building my voice."

"That seems a long time."

"I know. Christopher says the same thing. I don't think he approves of Mr. Sutton as a manager."

"Do you think Carroll's in love with Christopher?"

"Of course."

"Do you think she'll get him?"

"Only if Lisa deVita meets with an unfortunate accident." Heather looked at the stores that surrounded them. A man wearing a tuxedo was seated at a grand piano in the corridor, playing quiet melodies. "Know something? There are 55 shoe stores in the mall. Think that's enough choice?"

"Never too much choice in shoes!"

"I've got an idea! Let's window shop for our weddings."

They went into a store that sold bridal gowns and accessories. Mannequins were reflected along the mirrored walls, beautifully gowned for weddings they would never attend. A woman with a warm smile welcomed Heather and Liz, then left them alone to try on hats with veils and long white gloves.

"I like all the pearls," Heather said.

"And the lace."

"I know someone who's having eight bridesmaids when she marries."

"Eight?"

Heather nodded. "Remember that guy Chad?"

"I guess so! We've got a date tomorrow. You set it up, so don't forget to come!"

"I'll be there, don't you worry. Anyway, I've only met Chad once but he seemed friendly. I know his sister. She's the one who's having eight bridesmaids."

"Some wedding."

They decided to have lunch and walked to an outdoor cafe at the Ice Palace where the tables overlooked the ice. Heather and Liz ordered quiche Lorraine and spring water, then looked down at the rink.

"Hey," Liz said. "There's Chad."

He had curly black hair and was wearing an ice dancing costume. A female dancer and a grey-haired woman were with him on the ice. "She must be their coach," Liz said. She watched with fascination as Chad and the girl rehearsed with the woman, whirling around the ice. "I can't believe he's an ice dancer, and he's so good."

"Someone told me that's his cousin."

"His partner? That's great."

When the rehearsal ended they nibbled their quiche and a delicious salad while discussing the attack at the indoor sea. "You look for means, motive and opportunity," Liz said. "The villain has to have all three."

"So, who qualifies in the scuba club?"

Liz thought for a moment. "Well, any of them could have broken off a chunk of coral. So they all had the means, plus the opportunity."

"Don't they swim in buddies?"

"Sure, but two people could be in this together."

"You still need a motive."

Liz nodded. "I've been thinking about that. There's

been an underwater attack and a bomb left in Christopher's store. Both within 24 hours of each other. Why?"

"Some guy's got a grudge against Christopher."

"Or some woman. There's lots in that club." Liz thought for a minute. "What about someone not connected to the club? *Anyone* could have been underwater, waiting in the wreck for Christopher."

"You mean someone who got there early?"

"Sure, before the club members arrived. Quickly into scuba gear and quickly into the water. It's perfect, because of course the police would probably suspect the club members."

Liz saw a man approaching. He was wearing an old-fashioned suit that she thought was kind of strange. When he sat down at the table she remembered he was Mr. Sutton, Heather's manager.

He immediately began talking business. Heather smiled apologetically at Liz, then listened to Mr. Sutton's ideas about a road trip to Spokane and Seattle. As they talked Liz glanced at the nearby tank of piranhas and saw Christopher Dixon looking at the fish. Then he noticed her and smiled. As he walked over Mr. Sutton saw him approaching and stood up.

"Here comes the man with all the great ideas for your career. If you don't mind, Heather, I won't bother listening this time."

"But you just ordered strawberries and whipped cream."

"Share them with your friend." He pulled out some crumpled money and threw a bill on the table. "See you at rehearsal tonight. Be on time."

As he walked away Christopher sat down, smiling. "Two pretty faces! May I join you for a few minutes, before I get back to the store?"

"Sure," Heather said. "Are you okay after that attack?"

"Yes, but I'm certainly not going to just sit back and forget it happened."

"What do you mean?" Liz asked.

He turned to her with determined eyes. "I don't get mad, I get even. I'll find the person who slashed my air hose. That's a promise." He smiled at Heather. "Fabulous performance yesterday! Someone told me about it. The inside story is you're going to win the contest."

"Wouldn't that be great?"

"You're going to be a star, Heather. The only question is when. Tomorrow or five years from now?"

"Mr. Sutton says I need to build a strong foundation or I'll burn out fast. Kind of like a shooting star."

"Well, who knows? Mr. Sutton's made it clear that he doesn't like me or my advice. Maybe he's worked a long time in the music business but that doesn't mean you couldn't get a new manager."

"I suppose so."

"One more thing. Always think gold."

"You're a great cheering section."

"How's the food?" Christopher looked at the strawberries Mr. Sutton had ordered. He covered them with whipped cream and tried one. "Nice," he said, offering the dish to the girls. "I managed a restaurant near Sea World once. It had a nice view, but watching ice dancers while you eat is kind of unique." Turning from the rink he looked over Liz's shoulder at someone in the corridor, then glanced at his watch and put the strawberries down. Liz turned to see Carroll approaching with her father.

"Well," Carroll said, "here you are! I needn't have worried—just look for pretty girls and there you are. You should be back at work, Christopher."

He stood up. "Come on, Carroll. No need to stomp on me. Taking an extra five minutes isn't a major crime."

"You're right. Sorry, I'm really on edge."

As Christopher, Carroll and her father walked away Liz got out some money. "I'd like to know more about the McAndrews. Come on, Heather, let's pay our bill and see where they're going."

* * *

Soon they reached the indoor sea. There wasn't much of a crowd so only one sub was taking people on trips. A young attendant in a naval uniform saluted Mr. McAndrews as he went on board the sub with Carroll.

"Been on the trip?" Liz asked Heather.

"Sure, it's great."

"Feel like going again?"

"Okay."

They bought tickets and joined a small line of people on the dock. Then a hatch opened in the conning tower and Mr. McAndrews looked out.

"Hi sir," Liz said. "Can we get in that way?"

"Sorry, this is the emergency exit. Visitors enter through the hatch at the stern."

They went below to a double row of seats facing big portholes. As Liz and Heather sat down, Mr. McAndrews closed the emergency exit and stepped down into the cabin. Joining Carroll at the forward end of the sub he quietly spoke to her, while gesturing at various gauges.

"Why are they on board?" Liz said. "They're not tourists."

The stern hatch closed with a hollow thump. The air was warm and sweat beaded on Liz's forehead. She looked out at silver bubbles rising past the porthole, and saw an artificial crab clinging to the dock. Next to it she could see a fisherman's boot tangled in make-believe seaweed.

Mr. McAndrews looked at the passengers. "Good afternoon, folks!" He introduced himself and Carroll, then said he was in charge for this journey. "This will be a dangerous mission," he warned, as the sub moved slowly away from its berth. "We're going in search of the missing research sub, SR2."

The radio crackled as a voice said, *"You have clearance out of Bravo Bay, Admiral McAndrews."*

"Aye, aye," he replied. Then he looked at the others. "During the mission we'll be passing the ruins of Atlantis, that lost gem of civilization. We'll see fish from all over the world, perhaps even some sharks. Now everyone into position, and be watchful."

Liz and Heather leaned forward. They could see the portholes of another sub and its brass propeller. It was large and looked dangerous. They passed a circular glass tank in which little red fish swam, then saw a big grouper in its tank under the *Santa Maria*.

Mr. McAndrews was speaking quietly to his daughter, but she didn't seem to be listening. Instead, she was staring out a porthole, but wasn't concentrating on the view. Liz was sure something was troubling Carroll. But what could it be?

Everyone fell silent as the sub entered a tunnel. "Dangerous waters," Mr. McAndrews said ominously. "What's that to port? Is it the remains of the SR2?" Everyone leaned toward the left portholes, where they saw a make-believe sub crushed in the tentacles of a giant sea squid.

Suddenly Mr. McAndrews cried out. "We're under attack! We've lost our power!"

As the sub went dark someone screamed. Lights flashed on the control panel and Mr. McAndrews shouted excitedly about taking evasive action, then the sub glided out of the tunnel into peaceful waters. Mr. McAndrews was grinning after the adventure in the tunnel but Carroll's eyes were on the steel deck at her feet.

Liz looked out a porthole and saw the ghostly vision of the sunken wreck where Christopher's air hose had been slashed. She shivered, glad that he'd escaped with his life.

Then she looked toward the stern of the sub at a man in glasses who held a pocket notebook and pen.

He, too, was studying the wreck through a porthole. Determined to find out why, Liz stood up and walked toward the man.

7

The next morning Liz was shopping with her mother on Europa Boulevard. It was like a street in Paris, with pastel-coloured buildings side by side. Only a few people were on the tree-lined boulevard, but they were enjoying a great act in the Rock the Mall contest.

Rock Moves featured Ewan and Fiona Taft from British Columbia. They danced the length of the marble corridor, singing into small hand-held microphones while their band played under a street lamp that had hanging flower baskets.

After the act finished, Liz pulled her mother into a nearby store. "Know who owns this? One of the Edmonton Oilers! Maybe he'll be here."

The polished aluminum ceiling glowed with spotlights that shone on denim jackets and jeans. "Know what, Mom? They buy old clothes and turn them into these jeans and jackets." She smiled at the pretty girl behind the counter. "Hi, we're here to have lunch with Mark."

She laughed. "Take a number. You're the fourth girl today to try that act." She smiled at Mrs. Austen. "But I don't blame them for trying."

Mrs. Austen looked at a portrait of the handsome hockey player in his Oilers uniform. "If that's him I don't blame them, either."

"Will he be playing in the game Friday night?" Liz asked the girl.

"Unfortunately, no. He's at a celebrity golf tournament back east."

"Too bad." Liz tried on a jacket with a white satin kitten sewn on the back. "The game should be great, Mom. It's Edmonton against Calgary, but with only a few guys from each team, plus some local talent."

Back in the mall they looked in the window of a jewellery store at a necklace of miniature gold hearts and a ring inlaid with diamonds. "Who can afford all this?" Mrs. Austen said. "You'd need to own a money machine."

"Or a lot of credit cards." Liz went to the window of a nearby store where a pink hand-knit sweater graced a mannequin. "Can you imagine what would have happened if one of those bombs had gone off?"

"One more bomb or even a bomb scare, and we're heading home."

"Oh, Mom!"

"I know you love it here, sweetie, but I'm getting

nervous. That scuba diver could have drowned! I'll have to talk to your father."

Liz looked at two men cleaning the brass rails nearby. Tom had reported there were people who spent all day every day polishing them. Everything about the mall was so fantastic and now, suddenly, they might be going home.

"I still haven't found Aunt Melody a present. I'd better get it really fast."

Mrs. Austen smiled. "Don't sulk. Nothing's been decided."

Liz looked in a window. "Wow, Mom, there it is! The perfect gift for Aunt Melody." A tiny crystal piano turned slowly under a spotlight, dazzling her eyes with beams of coloured light. She hurried into the store, then left quickly after learning the price.

"Never mind," Mrs. Austen said. "It was a nice thought."

* * *

Near the rink they leaned over some stairs to look down at benches several floors below. People were changing into skates but Liz couldn't see Chad. "He's an ice dancer, you know."

Her mother smiled. "Yes, you've told us several times." She touched Liz's hair. "Time goes by so fast. Sometimes I wish you and Tom were back in diapers so we could watch you growing up again."

"*Diapers*? Mom, please! People might be listening." Liz glanced at the stairs, hoping Chad wasn't coming up from a rehearsal. "Please be more discreet with your comments, Mother. I *am* 16."

Laughing, they went into the International Market-place. It was like a narrow street in a foreign country, crowded with stalls selling dragons of pale green jade, tigers with gleaming fangs and the tiniest carved elephants they'd ever seen. There were also booths selling sugar baby mini-doughnuts, souvenirs of the mall and the chance to have your portrait taken in a gold rush outfit.

"Mom, a palm reader!" Liz pointed at the booth. "I have to know about my date with Chad!"

A bearded young man welcomed her to his table, then explained that reading her palm was like reading her mind. "The lines are like a map. I'll tell you what I discover."

They closed their eyes for two minutes, saying nothing. Then he studied her palms. "Your head line shows a thirst for knowledge. This trident means fame, fortune and honour if you follow your heart. But here," he said, pointing at a line, "I see confusion."

"You mean about what's been happening with the bombs? You're right, I'm really confused."

He shook his head. "Negative energy has entered your life recently. That's what's confusing."

"You mean someone I've met at the mall isn't very nice? Who?"

"I can't say that."

"What's going to happen?"

He smiled. "I'm not a fortune teller."

He continued with the reading, but Liz found it difficult to concentrate. Later, before having lunch with her mother, she stopped to throw a coin into a fountain. "Storm clouds are gathering. I can feel it in my bones."

"Storm clouds can't reach you, darling. This is an indoor city, remember?"

"There's more than one kind of storm."

As they entered Bourbon Street Liz looked at the shoeshine chairs, but Susan was gone. A small sign said CLOSED. A couple of people were talking at the far end of the street, but no one else moved under the lights that twinkled in the dark ceiling.

"I'm getting depressed," Liz said. "Maybe some food will help."

They chose a small table outside a café and were given menus. Mrs. Austen made her choice, then asked, "Heather arranged your date?"

"That's right. Her boyfriend knows Chad."

"He's seventeen. That's a year older than you."

"Don't worry, Mom, I'm not running away with him! It's just a minor little date, and Heather and her boyfriend will be with us."

"I don't call it minor when you're this excited." Mrs. Austen patted her hand. "Just remember one thing—you deserve the best."

"It'll be a great time! We're going to Galaxyland and then lunch and then the waterpark."

"Heather seemed very mature when I met her. Is that because of her music?"

"I think so. She travels a lot with her band, but she's also in university."

"In Edmonton?"

"Sure, she lives with her family. They're travellers, too. She was named Heather because her Dad loves Scotland."

"That's nice." Mrs. Austen waited for the waitress

to take Liz's order, then said, "Oysters for me."

"Oysters?" Liz stared at her. "Are you serious?"

"Of course. Besides, you had them in PEI."

"I had ONE oyster in PEI. The first and last of my life." Liz fiddled with a glass, then said, "I hope Heather wins."

"Why is a country band in a Rock the Mall contest?"

"Haven't you heard of k.d. lang? Heather's got the same sound."

"Oh. Well, I guess I'm out of touch."

"Heather could be a major star, but there may be a problem."

"What's that?"

"Her manager. That guy, Mr. Sutton. He's moving her career really slowly. Christopher says Heather should be performing in Nashville by now." She started her Caesar salad, then looked down Bourbon Street. "Hey, there's Mr. Sutton now. He's talking to Benn Dunn. Maybe he's a customer at the scuba store."

"He doesn't seem the type."

"You can never tell."

A few minutes later Benn Dunn walked toward the mall and Mr. Sutton came along the avenue. He looked up at the balcony where the first bomb had been discovered, then studied a New Orleans taxi parked on the cobblestones before finally noticing Liz. Slowly he came across the street, staring at her.

"Haven't I met you before?"

"Sure, with Heather." Liz introduced her mother, who invited Mr. Sutton to join them.

"Okay, but just for a few minutes. Heather's got a rehearsal downtown and I don't want to be late." He ordered a coffee, then smiled at Liz. "I bet you enjoy this place."

"That's for sure. But it's more fun when there's lots of people."

"Yeah, it looks like those bombs might have started to hurt business. But Mr. McAndrews has lots of money, so he'll survive. I was in the navy with him. After that he went into furniture and now expensive stores, and I went into the music business." He showed them a hole in his shoe. "That's been the story of my life, but now everything's going to be fine."

"Because of Heather?" Mrs. Austen asked.

"You bet. That's a golden voice, Mrs. Austen, and it means my big chance at last. I've had other good singers, but they peaked too fast. A single hit, then they fizzled out. By the time Heather hits the top she'll have a solid foundation. She'll be around a long time." He stirred his coffee with a plastic stick, then suddenly snapped it. "Certain people think I'm a bad manager for Heather. They think she should be an overnight sensation. That's bad advice."

"I'm sure that's true, Mr. Sutton."

"Believe me, Mrs. Austen, it's very true. Heather's going to the top and she's going there my way."

* * *

After lunch Liz and her mother went to the dolphin show. There were lots of seats, but only a scattering of spectators. Bright store signs reflected on the pool's green water, which was held back by a glass wall. The dolphins could be seen underwater, playing among the sunbeams, and then powering up to leap high above the waves.

Mr. McAndrews arrived to watch the show and joined them. "Good afternoon," he said, sitting down. "Attendance is pretty low today, isn't it? Management has decided to only run one sub ride." He looked at the yellow conning towers visible at their berth in the sea. "But that won't stop my morning journeys."

"What do you mean?"

"I'm ex-navy, Mrs. Austen. I was in subs for years until I decided to earn some real money in business. I've never lost my love for those things, so I've made a special arrangement with management. Every morning before the mall opens I go for a solo journey. Being all alone in that silent underwater world sets me up for the day."

"How do you feel about the bomber?"

"A kook for sure. Nothing makes sense! Why bombs that don't explode? Why the scuba attack? Why the silence from the bomber? No notes, no phone calls, no demands for a huge payoff. It's beginning to drive me crazy."

"Something will happen soon. I'm sure of that."

"Does Carroll like subs, too?" Liz asked.

"Sure, my daughter loves being underwater. Scuba diving's her big hobby."

"But what about subs?"

"Well, she's not wild about them, but I've been taking her on trips, teaching her how the things work. I'd like her to follow in my footsteps at the mall." For a few minutes he looked at the dolphin pool before adding, "Unfortunately Carroll's got a mind of her own. She's spent time in the Caribbean and wants to go back there. She was never enthusiastic about me setting up a store for her. Now she wants out."

"That's a shame," Mrs. Austen said. "You must be feeling a bit down these days."

"You're right, and that's why I'm here to watch the dolphins. They always make me feel better. I think our show rivals the one at Sea World in San Diego."

A poolside door opened and Lisa deVita appeared beside a man Liz hadn't met. She clipped a tiny microphone to the N.Y. JETS sweatshirt she wore over her wet suit, and introduced herself. "With me is our chief trainer, Ken Nguyen. These dolphins were born in the Gulf of Mexico. They'll live to about thirty-five, right in this pool."

"Wow." Liz grinned at her mom. "Imagine spending your entire life at the West Edmonton Mall."

As Ken began telling the audience some information about the dolphins and how they lived, Lisa walked slowly around the edge of the pool, looking at Liz in the stands. "I remember now—you're the girl who requested a special tour. Come and meet Mavis." When Liz reached the pool she was given some instructions and then, as Lisa made circling motions, a dolphin rose out of the water to be patted. "Wow," Liz exclaimed as she hurried back to her mother. "What an experience—her skin's rubbery and she smiled at me!"

Mrs. Austen hugged her. "They've got your kind of spirit, darling. No wonder I enjoy watching this show."

Some of the dolphins' stunts were spectacular and they were applauded enthusiastically by the small crowd as the show ended with them circling the pool on their sides, slapping the surface with grey flippers.

"I want that trainer's job," Liz grinned. "I wonder what's backstage?"

"Maybe you'll find out. She's waving you forward."

Within minutes arrangements had been made for a tour, which Mrs. Austen declined. "I brought some paperwork from Winnipeg that I haven't finished, so I think I'll get back to it."

"Your mom's nice," Lisa said, as she opened the door to an inner pool. "We can isolate a dolphin here for a medical examination."

"Do you ever swim with them?"

"Whenever I get the chance."

"What's it like?"

"They're shy. They circle around, watching, zapping out their sound waves. After a while they start playing."

"Lisa, may I ask you a personal question?"

"Sure. What do you need to know?"

"Are you engaged to Christopher?"

"Well, I'm not sure. He's talked about marriage, but so far no ring and no announcements. My family's getting restless. They want to start planning the wedding." She laughed. "I'm not *that* anxious, but I hate uncertainty."

"How's Carroll fit in?"

"She worries me. I hate to say it, but maybe she's the reason for no ring."

"She's moved in on Christopher?"

"Kind of. When he first started working at the mall as a guide he joined our scuba club. We started dating. Then Carroll came home from a long holiday in the Caribbean. One look at Christopher and, bingo, he was the manager of her new store."

"Has he dated her?"

"No, but he's a natural flirt. That just encourages Carroll. I try to act like I don't care, but I do."

In another room Lisa filled a pail with dead squid. "You know something? When Christopher's air hose got slashed I was really upset for him. But something else bothers me."

"What's that?"

"My scuba outfit is identical to Christopher's, and I swam through the wreck just before he did." She looked at Liz with huge, dark eyes. "I think the attack was meant for me."

* * *

Ten minutes later Liz was still asking questions, but Lisa couldn't offer any proof. "It's just a feeling," she said. "But I'm nervous anyway."

"Have you told the police?"

"Sure. They wrote it down, but that's all."

Walking down some metal stairs, they entered a corridor where their voices echoed, and there were pipes and air-conditioning ducts high above. After following a confusing route they reached an open space with a low ceiling and concrete walls. Before them was a huge tank, with waves moving on the restless surface.

"I'm nervous," Liz said. "Where are we?"

"Don't worry, we're perfectly safe." The trainer stepped onto a platform above the tank. Reaching into her pail, she tossed dead squid in different directions. The water erupted immediately as thick snouts burst forth, revealing razor-sharp teeth that tore the squid and slashed at each other's hides. As Lisa continued to throw squid Liz stared in horror at the sharks fighting each other for the food, then said, "I'll wait in the corridor."

"Okay."

Eventually Lisa joined her, smiling cheerfully. "These are only lemon sharks, you know, not great whites."

"Sure Lisa, but they're scary anyhow. Scary, scary, scary."

Lisa collected another pail of food and they went upstairs to the mall to feed the fish in the *Santa Maria*'s tank. At the railing around the sea they looked across the water at the galleon.

"See that two-headed serpent?" Liz pointed at the bow. "It's really bad luck for the *Santa Maria*."

"But it'll never be in a storm."

"That serpent is still bad news." Liz looked at the crow's nest high above. "Imagine if one of those Spanish sailors came through a time warp to the present. What would he think of the view from up there now?"

"That he'd really found a new world," Lisa laughed. "You've got an imagination like mine."

Christopher had arranged to meet Lisa, and was waiting as they approached the *Santa Maria*. He kissed her, then smiled at Liz. "How's the bomb investigation?"

"Slow."

"I'm close to learning something. I already have a name, but I need proof."

"*Who is it?*"

"Sorry, not yet. But I should know something soon."

Lisa put her arms around Christopher and looked up

into his blue eyes. "Please, Chris, be careful. I get so worried."

He hugged her, then looked at Liz. "You were just at the shark feeding?"

"Yes, but how'd you know?"

"Your face is still the colour of chalk. Those sharks give me the creeps, too, but Lisa loves them. She's crazy about anything that swims."

Liz looked at the dark entrance to the sub tunnel. "What's that steel catwalk for?"

"It runs the length of the tunnel. If a sub ever got stuck in there the passengers could escape out the conning tower, then follow the catwalk to the mall."

"Any chance of taking a look in the tunnel?"

"Sure."

Their voices were muffled in the darkness. Cool air blew from air-conditioning ducts and the black water was calm. Liz imagined a sub moving silently past, the orange light flashing on its conning tower.

"I wonder . . ."

"What?" Lisa asked.

"Just . . . well, what if a sub did stop in here? Someone could sneak out the conning tower and into the water in scuba gear. No one in the mall would see."

"But why do that?"

"I'm not sure. It's just an idea."

Outside the tunnel they walked to the *Santa Maria*. As Liz stepped onto the deck a cloud crossed the sun, throwing a dark shadow across the galleon. She shivered and was glad when the others joined her. The sun returned, but soon they descended a ladder into more darkness.

"This is the hold of the *Santa Maria*," Lisa said, switching on a bare lightbulb. The yellow glow showed a floor of rough planks and a low ceiling. There were shadows all around. Below them was a tank lit up by hidden lights, where exotic fish moved among the green ferns.

"It's nice and cool in here."

"The *Santa Maria*'s connected to the mall's air conditioning system."

"Those groupers are something. Only a mother could love a face like that."

"How about the stingrays? I've petted one."

"Better you than me." Liz looked at the tank's glass wall. "That's the sea out there, right?"

Lisa nodded. "People in the sub can see these fish."

"I was on that trip just yesterday." Liz hesitated, then added, "Mr. McAndrews was on the sub. So was Carroll."

She watched Christopher closely, but he didn't react to the woman's name. He was looking into the tank, watching a grouper patrol its territory. But Lisa turned to look at Liz.

"Funny you should mention Carroll," she said. "I was just thinking about challenging her to a duel. We could fight it out underwater. Spearguns at 50 flipper-paces, or something like that."

"Are you still jealous of her?" Christopher asked.

"I didn't think it showed." Lisa looked up at him. "Don't you think it would be an interesting duel?"

There was a smile on her lips, but not in her eyes.

8

In Tom's hotel room he lay on the floor, reading. Dietmar was watching TV. He was sprawled on the bed, which was in the back of a Ford pickup truck. There was a smaller bed in the cab, and a traffic cop stood over the Jacuzzi. On the walls and ceiling were traffic signs and lights.

Dietmar turned off the television. "You know Europa Boulevard?"

"Of course. We were there an hour ago."

"Oh yeah, I forgot. Anyway, I . . ."

"That boulevard is like Paris."

"You mean with all those balconies? You know, I've been thinking about them. That would be a long fall."

"Sick, Oban."

Dietmar jumped off the bed. "Listen, how about playing Pebble Beach? My treat."

"What's going on? You hate golf and you never buy for me."

"Not true, Austen. Anyway, how about it?"

"Sure, okay." Tom closed his book. "Let's get going."

"I'm not quite ready. I need 30 minutes, okay?"

"Why?"

"I met this girl, and I want to invite her. I'm going to her mother's store to ask her."

"Use the phone."

Dietmar shook his head. "I'll walk. I need the exercise." He went into his room, which was connected to Tom's, and closed the door. For several minutes Tom heard him moving around, then all was quiet. He thought about the girl Dietmar wanted to invite, then turned on the television.

He was watching a game show when the phone rang. "Tom," Dietmar exclaimed. "It's me."

Tom sat up. "What's wrong?"

"I'm in Europa Boulevard! I think I know who the bomber is! Meet me here as soon as . . ."

"Dietmar, who is it?"

"Not over the phone! Get down here fast!"

"Where will you be?"

"I'm not sure, but look for a woman with red hair. She's my contact and . . ."

The line went dead.

Tom stared at the phone, then hung up fast. Grabbing his room key, he raced down the hallway to the elevators.

As he waited, jiggling the key in his hand and pacing the carpet, he was joined by an elderly couple.

"Canada's such a different country," the lady said to

Tom. "There's no hotel like this back home."

"Where you from, boy?" the man asked.

"Winnipeg."

He held out a hand. "So was my Granddaddy. Shake, cousin."

Finally the elevator reached the lobby. Tom raced to the indoor sea, flew past the *Santa Maria* and up the escalator to Europa Boulevard.

But there was no sign of Dietmar. At the far end of the boulevard someone sat under the hanging flower baskets of a Victorian lamp-standard, but no one else was around. Tom walked slowly past a store with denim jackets in the window, then looked back toward the *Santa Maria*. Where was Dietmar?

Suddenly a scream rang out.

Where had it come from? Tom turned, staring, as people ran out from several stores. Then a sales assistant pointed up.

"There! On that balcony!"

Tom looked at the top of an elegant old building. Something or someone was up there. He could see a big mop of red hair.

"Don't jump," he yelled. "I'm coming up! I'll help you."

But it was too late. The figure leaned out further and everyone saw a T-shirt with wide stripes of vivid colours. The crowd screamed and scattered as the figure toppled off the balcony and fell, tumbling through the air to smash into the marble corridor.

Running forward, Tom looked at the victim.

Blue buttons for eyes. The nose a black button. A mop for hair.

Everyone was staring at him. "Hey, this isn't my gag." Tom raised defensive hands. "Don't blame me. I'm not involved."

There were some angry mutterings, until a sales assistant laughed. "Let's relax, folks! It made a real change from a boring day. I'll phone the custodians to clean it up."

Tom decided to tell Neil Raj about the fake suicide, and hurried through the mall to Luggage Unlimited.

His friend laughed as he heard about Dietmar. "He picked the perfect time for it, with the mall so deserted. On a normal evening he could have injured some shopper or a tourist."

"You closing now?"

Neil Raj looked at his watch. "Five minutes."

"Great. How about the Mindbender? Should we . . ."

Neil Raj looked out the window. "Not again!" He smashed his hand against the counter top. "When will it end?"

The boys in the leather jackets were back. Two of them stayed in the corridor, while the Skull came into the store. Without saying anything he stared at them.

"Something I can do for you?" Neil Raj said.

The Skull shook his head. He walked to a display of attaché cases and studied one, then dropped it on the floor. He kicked it to one side, then dropped a second case.

"Please leave the store," Neil Raj said.

A nine-year-old boy came in the door. He had some money in his hand. "Hi," he said cheerfully. "I want a present for my mom's birthday."

Tom looked at the Skull, who was staring at the boy. Neil Raj said, "Sorry, but the store's closed."

The boy looked at his watch. "The sign says you close at nine. That gives me two minutes."

"Nothing I can do about that." Neil Raj smiled regretfully. "You can't come in."

"False advertising! Our teacher told us about that."

With a tight smile on his face, Neil Raj escorted the boy out of the store. He watched until he was safely down the corridor, then came inside and looked at the Skull. "Okay, I'll say it again. It's time for you to leave."

The Skull reached inside his leather jacket and took out a can of spray paint. Neil Raj walked quickly to the phone, but the Skull leapt forward and ripped the cord from the wall. For a moment the two faced each other, then Neil Raj glanced at Tom. "Let's go. I'll phone security from one of their hot lines in the mall."

As his friend walked out of the store Tom saw the Skull looking at a picture on the wall. It was a family portrait of Neil Raj and his parents. Raising his hand, the Skull sprayed red paint across the picture.

Tom sprang at the Skull, hitting his wrist with a karate blow. The paint can fell to the floor and bounced away.

"You stupid . . ."

The Skull looked out the window. Neil Raj had stopped a security guard in the corridor and was gesturing toward the store. As soon as the guard spoke into his two-way radio the Skull's friends melted away around a corner.

"There goes your army," Tom said. "You've had it."

The Skull ran toward the back of the store. Tom

hesitated, then realized the guard couldn't reach the store in time to catch him. Running swiftly through the upper display area, he raced into the storage room.

There was no sign of the Skull.

Tom couldn't find the light switch. In the gloom a machine was running with a low hum, a tap dripped and someone was breathing. Tom walked forward and, just as he'd found the switch, something was smashed across the back of his head. With a cry he fell to the floor, and lay shaking his head trying to fight the pain.

Looking up, he saw the Skull above. He'd reached the top of a shelf and was pushing away a ceiling tile. Just as the Skull pulled himself up into the darkness Tom staggered to his feet and started to climb the shelves to the ceiling. The air was musty as he pulled himself into the crawlspace. Faint light glowed from stores below and he could hear the crackle of the security guard's two-way radio as the man ran into the luggage store.

"Up here," Tom yelled. "In the crawlspace."

Then he heard the Skull, scrambling away into the darkness. Moving cautiously, Tom followed the sound until he saw a dim shape ahead.

"Take off," the Skull hissed. "I've got a knife."

"I doubt it. You'd have used it before now."

"*Take off!*"

"You're caught. There's spray paint on your fingers and three witnesses, including that kid. Maybe you . . ."

The Skull came at him out of the darkness, hands outstretched and snarling. They fell together, fighting until a flashlight beam cut the darkness. "Over here,"

Tom yelled to the security guard as he pinned the Skull to the floor. "You stupid jerk! You're finished now."

9

After being questioned by the police, Tom walked through the empty corridors toward the hotel.

The mall was a different world with all the stores closed. Behind the glass wall of an aviary a flamingo stood on one leg watching him with a tiny eye, while others slept with their beaks buried in pink feathers. At the indoor sea spotlights glowed under the dark surface, revealing the shapes of broken statues and the outline of the wreck where Christopher had come close to losing his life. After walking to the end of the sea, Tom followed a path among bushy plants to a railing at the water's edge. Beneath the surface he could see the sharks circling in their brightly lit tank, a strange and frightening sight in the silence of the mall.

Back at the hotel he found his parents pacing the floor.

They were pretty upset and were telling him exactly what they thought when Dietmar walked in with a happy grin. "Hiya, Austen! What happened in Europa . . ?"

Mrs. Austen held up a hand. "Hold it right there, Dietmar. We've just had a call from Mr. McAndrews. He heard about your stunt in Europa Boulevard and wants you sent home."

Dietmar turned pale. "Really?"

Mrs. Austen nodded. "It took all my courtroom skills to change his mind."

Grinning, Dietmar shook her hand. "You're a pal."

"You may not think so tomorrow."

* * *

Soon after the stores opened next morning Mrs. Austen returned to the suite with a pizza-shaped container and sent Tom to wake Dietmar. It was a long time before the two returned.

"This guy sleeps like he's in a coma. I could have driven a fire engine past the bed without him noticing."

Dietmar yawned. "I watched movies until six a.m., and I can hardly see."

"I've just bought a present for you, Dietmar."

"Thanks, Mrs. A. What did it cost?"

Tom snorted. "Do you measure everything in dollars, Oban? Sometimes you act like you're only a bit smarter than a bag of nails."

Mrs. Austen gave Dietmar the container. "Like so many things in the mall, this holds a world record."

"I've eaten bigger pizzas, Mrs. Austen."

"Just open it."

Dietmar cracked the lid to reveal an enormous cookie with writing on it that said *You're grounded.* "You've got to be kidding!"

"Care to bet on that?"

"Do I get to eat the cookie?"

"As long as you don't forget the message."

"Great! My favourite game show's on this morning, so I'll eat this thing while I watch it." He looked at Tom. "Call for me around two, and we'll go to the waterpark."

Mrs. Austen raised a hand. "Dietmar, you'd better turn that cookie over."

He gave it a spin, then stared at the words written on the back: *for two days.* "Grounded for two days? But we're at the West Edmonton Mall!"

"Next time you'll be grounded for life."

* * *

An hour later Liz arrived outside Galaxyland for the double date. Heather was with her boyfriend, Marc Hewitt. He was good looking and so was Liz's date, Chad Fleetwood, who was a nice dresser and wore a jacket with the name of his skating club on the back.

Inside the amusement park, Liz looked at the boats on the small lake, and at the miniature train. "This place is truly amazing. Imagine having an entire amusement park inside a shopping mall."

"You're right," Chad said. "And the Mindbender's waiting for us."

"The triple-loop roller coaster? I'm not crazy about riding that."

"You'll love it."

"I've done it once. That felt like enough."

Heather and Marc wanted to ride the Orbitron so they agreed to try that first. Soon they were experiencing massive acceleration. Their cars rapidly rose and fell, bouncing them up and down, forward and back, as the girls screamed and their hair whipped around their faces. "Wow," Liz gasped when the ride ended, "that was great!"

At the washroom she and Heather combed their hair and checked themselves in the mirror. "I can tell Chad likes you," Heather said. "You're doing great."

Liz grinned. "I'm a nervous wreck."

"Just relax and enjoy yourself."

After riding the bumper cars and winning a couple of plush velvet animals, they reached the Drop of Doom. Looking like the steel structure that stands beside space rockets at the launch pad, it rose high above.

Chad turned to Liz. "Scared of that thing?"

"No. Why?"

"The Mindbender scares you."

"Where'd you get that?"

"You're afraid to ride it."

"That's not what I said."

"Good, because that's what we're doing after this ride."

Liz looked at his blue eyes. "Maybe I'll do it. I haven't decided yet."

"Not maybe," Chad replied. "For sure."

Liz turned toward the Drop of Doom. "Come on, I'll buy this one."

"Nope I'll get the tickets." Pulling out his money,

Chad walked to the booth and soon they were being strapped into a small cage at the foot of the steel structure.

"Good luck," the attendant said. "Imagine you're about to step off a 120-storey building. That's what the ride feels like." Grinning, he stepped back. "I'll give you a free second ride if you survive this one."

Suddenly the cage began to rise. For a moment Liz closed her eyes, then looked down. Far below, a solitary tourist was aiming a video camera in their direction. Quickly the woman grew smaller then with a crash the cage stopped at the top of the blue steel.

Rolling forward on small wheels, it stopped over eternity. Liz moaned, then everything fell away as the cage plunged down, faster and faster, while the metal wheels roared in their tracks and soundless screams erupted from her throat.

Suddenly the cage changed direction and slammed to a stop. As the attendant leaned into the cage to release them he asked, "Going up again?"

"Forget it," Chad groaned. "My stomach's still on the 95th floor."

"I won't argue with you," Liz said as they staggered away from the ride to join Heather and Marc. "That thing's a killer."

"The Mindbender's next."

Liz looked at the nearby roller coaster. The triple-loops rose so high that it was difficult to see their tops. While she watched, a red car came swiftly out of a loop, its riders screaming with delight, then roared straight back up into the heavens.

"Wicked."

"I'll get the tickets," Chad said.

"I don't think I'll go." Liz pointed at a nearby bench. "I'll wait here for you guys. Watch for me waving!"

"Hold it." Chad raised a hand. "You're riding the Mindbender."

"You keep ordering me to ride the thing. What if I don't want to?"

"You're with me."

"Hey," Liz said, her voice trembling. "Hey, this is turning into a mess. I'll just go sit down."

"If you do," Chad said, "the party's over." He stared at her, saying nothing more. His eyes were a vivid blue, with wonderful long lashes.

"Listen," Liz said. "This is getting crazy. I'll sit this ride out, okay? I'll see you guys after it."

"Forget it. You're coming with us."

Liz looked at Heather and Marc. They were watching, and so were several other people. "Come on, let's drop this insane argument. Okay?"

"It's not okay," Chad said. "I spent a lot of money on you today."

For a moment Liz was quiet. She looked at him, then at Heather and Marc. Suddenly her whole body shook with anger. "Here," she said, pulling some money from her pocket. "Here's a refund."

Chad stared at her without saying a word. Then he turned and disappeared in the direction of the roller coaster. Liz turned to Marc and Heather.

"I've gotta go. See you tomorrow, okay?"

"Sure, but . . ."

"Can't talk! Sorry!"

Liz hurried through the amusement park on legs like rubber. She didn't see or hear anything, she just walked fast, wanting to get out of Galaxyland. At last she reached the mall and saw people looking in store windows. As she walked along the polished marble, thinking about Chad, she saw some fountains ahead. They seemed to be dancing in time to the Blue Danube Waltz.

"Wow," she whispered as she watched the water. "I'm *really* glad I did that!"

10

That evening Tom and Liz were eating in a huge arcade, surrounded by booths that sold food from many places. There was salad from Greece, tortillas from Mexico and teri yaki from Japan, but they were eating hamburgers from McDonald's.

"So," Liz said, "do you think I did the right thing?"

"Of course! That guy's a jerk. What did Heather say?"

"She phoned my room an hour ago. She said she was really sorry it happened, but she thinks what I did was great."

Tom looked at his watch. "Hey, it's getting late. All the good places will be taken."

"Too bad Dietmar's still grounded. I bet he's sorry he has to miss this."

Mr. McAndrews was among the people walking

through the mall to the Ice Palace. "This is great," he said to Tom and Liz. "An exciting game and more crowds than I've seen since the bombs started."

"I hear Cayley Wilson's playing tonight," Tom said. "Is that true?"

"You bet. I organized this game as a summer exhibition and Cayley said he'd play. So are some of the other Oilers, and several players from the Calgary Flames. They all agreed to play despite the bomber."

"Could you get me Cayley Wilson's autograph?" Tom asked.

"I can do better than that. How'd you like to meet him?"

"I guess so!"

Mirrored stairs led down to a basement area with Coke and video machines lining the walls, a skate shop, and doors leading to various dressing rooms. One of them featured the Oilers' logo; Mr. McAndrews went inside and returned a minute later with Cayley Wilson. He was tall, with blond hair and green eyes.

"It's good to meet you," he said with a friendly handshake. "Mr. McAndrews tells me you're crime busters."

"Sort of," Tom said, while Liz smiled shyly.

"What's been your biggest case so far?"

They talked for a while, then Cayley signed autographs and returned to the dressing room to prepare for the game. After thanking Mr. McAndrews, Tom and Liz followed some stairs that curved up to the Oilers' bench, beside the rink.

"Look at the crowd!"

The railings on both levels were jammed with fans.

Most waved OILERS banners, but there were a lot of red flags being waved by Flames' supporters who'd driven north from Calgary. Tom and Liz went through a low gate into the crowd and managed to work their way to Heather's side. She'd saved them places by the railing.

"What excitement!" she grinned. "I bet this is better than a Stanley Cup final."

A roar from the crowd greeted the Oilers as they stepped on the ice, followed by the Flames. A few announcements were made, then Mr. McAndrews dropped a ceremonial puck and left the ice, waving to the crowd with his stetson.

Within seconds the play was directly in front of them. Two players fought for the puck in the corner, then it sprang loose toward Cayley. Picking it up behind the net, he began a move to the right. Then, in mid stride, he changed direction and broke to his left. The Calgary goalie was taken off-balance and watched helplessly as Cayley slipped the puck into the net.

The Ice Palace erupted with cheers from the Oilers' fans. People all around the rink yelled and stamped their feet and waved flags until the action resumed. Then, just after the players had swept past Tom, he looked at the upper railing and realized he was being watched.

Leaning close to Liz he whispered, "Someone's staring at us. Upper railing in sunglasses. Is that a wig he's wearing?"

"The one carrying the skates? It could be a she in that bulky coat."

"I think it's a he. Why's he watching us, not the game?"

"She's leaving."

The person in sunglasses pushed through the crowd to the glass-walled elevator. It descended to the lower level, then the strange figure disappeared down the curving stairs toward the dressing rooms.

Heather looked at them. "Hey, you're missing all the action! This is a fantastic game."

"Would you save our place?"

"Okay, but it won't be easy."

The Oilers on the bench were leaning forward, watching every move. The noise of cheering was really loud as Tom and Liz followed the stairs down to the changing area. It was empty.

"Is she in the skate shop?" Liz asked.

Tom tried the door. "Locked. What about the dressing room?"

"Also locked." Liz glanced up the mirrored stairs that led above. "There, look!"

The person in sunglasses was at the top of the stairs. One hand held a skate, the other was adjusting dark curls. "That's a wig for sure," Tom said. "Who is he?"

"And why did she come down here?"

"The skates! He's only got one now!"

"Then where's the other one? Is it hidden down here?"

Quickly they looked under benches and on the tops of the video games without finding it, then noticed the skate sharpener. Tom raced to the machine, fumbling for coins, and soon the small door slowly opened to reveal a skate within. A ticking sound could be heard and wires were visible inside the skate.

"The red one's connected! This isn't a false alarm!"

"We've got to warn people."

Tom and Liz raced to the stairs that curved up to the Oilers' bench, where they found Cayley Wilson wiping his face with a towel. "Calgary just tied the score," he said. "Why were you downstairs? You're missing a great game."

As soon as Tom explained, Cayley swung over the boards onto the ice. The referee blew his whistle, signalling a penalty, but Cayley quickly skated over to the announcer's booth and grabbed the microphone.

"Sorry folks," he said through the speakers, "but the game's over." There were a few groans, then everyone fell silent. "There's a bomb threat. Please leave the area immediately."

* * *

Tom and Liz were soon back at their parents' hotel suite watching television coverage of the incident. The cream-coloured outside walls of the supermall were shown on TV as the cameras panned over the watching crowds and the many police vehicles. Finally, Inspector Winter Eagle made the announcement everyone was waiting for.

"The bomb has been safely defused, thanks to Inspector Ted Austen of the Winnipeg Police."

"When will you make an arrest?" a reporter shouted.

"I've just issued a warrant."

"What? You're about to arrest someone? Who?"

"I can't reveal that."

As the questions continued Mr. Austen came into the room. He kissed his wife and gave her a big hug, then looked at Tom and Liz. "Pack your bags, kids.

You're going home."

"I was afraid of that," Tom said.

"I've been checking flight times," Mrs. Austen said to her husband. "The first plane is tomorrow afternoon."

Mr. Austen congratulated Tom and Liz for discovering the bomb. "Want to know something strange? That thing wouldn't have exploded for six hours."

"Did the bomber need that much time to escape?"

"Possibly, but that's a long wait in the skate sharpener. Anyone might have found the bomb." Mr. Austen loosened his tie. "We found initials inside the skate."

"What were they?"

"B. D."

"Benn Dunn!"

Mr. Austen nodded. "He worked in the store where a bomb was discovered, he was Christopher Dixon's scuba partner when the air hose was slashed, and when we ran his name through the computer earlier, we found out that he's served time in prison. The police have issued a warrant for his arrest."

The phone rang. After a brief conversation Mr. Austen hung up, shaking his head. "That was Inspector Winter Eagle. The police went to Benn Dunn's store to make the arrest, but he was gone. Then they tried his apartment."

"What did they find?"

"Nothing." Mr. Austen looked at them. "Benn Dunn has disappeared."

* * *

"Our last morning at the West Edmonton Mall!" Liz stared at the long corridors of marble, trees and fountains. "Our last walk to the World Waterpark."

Tom nodded. "We're lucky Dietmar broke Mom and Dad's hearts with his plea to say farewell to the waterslides."

"That's right, Austen," Dietmar grinned. "You owe me."

Passing the submarine dock they waved at Mr. McAndrews as he lifted the hatch on the conning tower. Climbing down a ladder, the man disappeared into the sub to begin his solitary morning journey around the indoor sea. "What a lonely guy," Liz said. "I feel sorry for him."

Outside the locker rooms they met Neil Raj, who thanked Tom again for his help at the luggage store and invited them to his house to try a curry dinner. "The best you've ever eaten! I'll make it myself."

"At 1:00 P.M.," Tom said mournfully, "our jet takes off for Winnipeg."

Dismayed by the news, Neil Raj looked solemn as they entered the humid air of the waterpark. No volleyball players were on the big court; at the ping-pong tables there was only one pot-bellied man who called *wanna game?* but they turned down the offer and continued to the beach.

Not a single person lay under the palm trees or rode the inner tubes of the Raging Rapids. Three teenagers waited in the wave lake for a blasting horn to announce *surfs up*, but their cheer was nothing to the usual delighted yells of the waiting mobs of surfers.

"What a pathetic scene," Liz said.

"I don't know about that." Dietmar pointed high in the air. "There's no waiting for the Sky Screamer."

Neil Raj looked at the others. "Who's your fastest?"

"Him," Tom said, looking at Dietmar. "Believe it or not."

"Want a race?"

"Of course."

At the highest platform, nine stories above the wave lake, the swimmers below looked like ants. "What a drop," Liz said, staring at the double-tracked Sky Screamer that fell a long way straight down. "You guys can go first."

With a happy smile Neil Raj stepped forward. When Dietmar had swung onto the twin slide, Liz gave them a countdown. Then, with rebel yells, they dropped from sight.

Tom watched the water below explode into a million crystal diamonds as the pair hit the splash-down pool. Jumping on the slide, he looked at Liz on the other path.

"Let's go!"

Feet together, hands behind his head, Tom dropped into emptiness. For a few heart-stopping seconds he was free falling, then he made contact again with the slide while plunging straight down with the wind screaming in his ears. At the bend he winced as his feet hit the water and the first silver bullets slammed into his sinuses, then he was in the pool, swimming toward the others waiting on the deck.

"Who won?"

Neil Raj laughed. "Dietmar broke my personal best.

When we saw our times on the scoreboard I couldn't believe my eyes."

Dietmar shrugged modestly. "By the way, Austen, you also lost . . . to your own sister."

Tom glanced at the results on the scoreboard. Avoiding Liz's eyes he said, "Which slide next?"

"Let's play some volleyball. I saw a ball lying on the court."

Within minutes they'd been joined by the pot-bellied man and a few other people, and soon after that the ball was spiked off Dietmar's head by Liz. He kicked it at her but missed, and they watched the ball fly into a stand of nearby trees.

"Nice move, Gomer." Liz ran into the trees and then reappeared to call, "Hey, Tom. Come and look at this."

The other boys ran with him into the trees. Liz stood over an opening in the ground. Cool air blew into their faces. "The ball fell into this air conditioning duct," Liz said. "See it down there beside that package?"

Tom and Liz dropped into the opening. Standing with their heads just below ground level, they glanced through a metal grill into the darkness of the duct, and then Tom bent to examine the package.

"It's a bomb!" He looked up at Neil Raj and Dietmar. "Call security on a hot line phone." As they disappeared he turned to Liz. "How'd the bomber get this package here?"

"Through the duct?" She shook the screen and it fell open. "Look, the hinges have been cut with a hacksaw. I bet this is how the bomber's been sneaking around the mall."

Tom looked into the darkness. "What do you think?"

"I'm not sure. It's so black in there."

"Maybe . . ." Tom stared at his sister. "Did you hear that?"

"Yes!"

They crawled into the duct, then waited. Seconds later the sound came again. Somewhere in the darkness a voice was shouting for help.

11

Tom moved further into the black duct with Liz right behind him. The metal was cold and there was just enough room for them to crawl slowly forward. Again the cries for help sounded, followed by silence.

Tom and Liz continued on for some time. To the right was a wire-mesh grill; through it they saw the orange light on the conning tower of a submarine. "I think it's in the tunnel," Liz whispered. "But it isn't moving."

"I hear a thumping sound. Somebody's kicking a wall or something."

Tom and Liz moved toward the sound. They turned a final bend in the air-conditioning duct, then climbed a short ladder to another dark space. Slivers of light leaked in through cracks in a wooden wall. The faint light showed a man tied to the wall. A piece of cloth had been shoved into his mouth. As Tom tore it away he recognized Benn Dunn. His eyes were desperate as he gasped, "Quick you kids! You've only got a few minutes. There's a bomb at my feet, set to explode. Go through that opening in the wall and set Mr. McAndrews free, then he'll get me out of this mess."

"Set him free? What's that mean?"

"Shut up and get moving! I don't want to die!"

Tom and Liz raced to a narrow space that led between rough boards. Not knowing what lay ahead, they followed the darkness until Tom's hand touched a dark velvet curtain. Pushing it aside, he saw more slivers of faint light. In the centre of an open space was a large tank where fish could be seen; stingrays, groupers and tarpin. Above the surface of the tank Mr. McAndrews hung from a rope around his chest: his hands and feet were tied, his mouth was gagged, and he had a blindfold over his eyes. The big man twisted slowly on the rope that led from the roof to the wall, where it was attached to a bracket.

Near the bracket stood someone in a scuba outfit, face hidden behind a mask and head covered by black rubber. Hearing Tom and Liz, the unknown person turned in their direction, holding a speargun.

With a gesture, they were ordered forward. Tom went to the left of the tank, Liz immediately went right. The figure in black was forced to swivel the speargun back and forth, trying to keep them both covered. Then a blast of sound came from somewhere distant, vibrating the glass of the tank and making the tarpin flash into hiding. At the bottom of the tank, beside its glass wall, Tom noticed a package among the ferns.

Then he saw the shark.

Coming from distant water, it moved swiftly in his direction. As it reached the glass wall below and turned away, a second shark appeared. Then, at last, Tom realized a bomb had torn open their tank, freeing the sharks. They were in the sea now, and would get into the tank below if the package near the wall exploded. After that, it would be only a matter of time until Mr. McAndrews was attacked.

Just then there was a muffled cry as Liz crashed into the figure in the scuba suit, hitting the black shape from behind and knocking the speargun into the tank. Tom managed to grab the gun; lifting it clear of the water, he threw it to Liz as the black shape came at him. Then, as they struggled, Liz loomed above, pointing the speargun at the mask.

"Leave my brother alone," she shouted. "I know how to work this gun."

Tom broke free of the strong hands as they were raised in surrender. Racing around the tank, he grabbed the rope and pulled with all his strength. It was on several pulleys so he was able to raise Mr. McAndrews a short distance and then . . .

BLAM!!

Water flew everywhere as the tank was blown apart. Tom was knocked down, but managed to keep his grip on the rope. Struggling to his feet, he raised Mr. McAndrews a bit higher as a shark smashed its way into the shattered tank. A stingray was helpless before it, and then a grouper fell victim to a second grey attacker.

Tom stared at the evil eyes of the sharks in the tank,

knowing that they'd soon see Mr. McAndrews dangling above. Then his sister cried out as the black figure broke away from her.

"Tom, I can't do it! I can't shoot that person! Look out!"

He only had a second to think, not knowing how to defend himself without dropping the rope. Then a spear slammed into the wall, briefly creating a barrier between Tom and the attacker.

Liz dropped the gun and ran to help pull Mr. McAndrews higher, just as a shark exploded from the water, its savage teeth coming menacingly close. Again they pulled as a second shark made a desperate bid, barely missing the man's feet. The black figure darted under the spear and tried to knock them away from Mr. McAndrews' lifeline, but they held on desperately, refusing to give up.

Out of the corner of his eye Tom saw feet appear on a nearby ladder that connected to somewhere above. With lightning speed a police woman in uniform came down the ladder with a gun.

"Don't move!" She carefully approached the figure in black, the gun steady in front of her. "There's reinforcements right behind."

"But," Liz said, "how'd you get here so fast?"

"We were already at the mall because of the bomb in the waterpark. Someone heard the blast under the *Santa Maria* and alerted us." As other officers came down the ladder she pulled the scuba mask off the attacker's face and Liz cried out in shock.

"I don't believe it. Christopher!"

* * *

Liz was still recovering an hour later. She sat on the deck of the *Santa Maria*, leaning against a cannon. Tom was nearby, listening to the questions being asked of Christopher Dixon. The blond man was in handcuffs. He sat near the open hatch leading to the ship's hold below, where the sharks had nearly ended Mr. McAndrews' life.

The police had arrived in time to save Benn Dunn from the bomb in the forward hold of the *Santa Maria*. "Tell me again," Inspector Winter Eagle said to Christopher. "You built a secret headquarters in the empty forward hold, but how did you get all the bomb materials into there?"

"I volunteered to help Lisa feed the fish. When we went on board the *Santa Maria* I was often carrying a package, but Lisa didn't notice how many times I left the ship without it." He smiled without warmth. "Later I crawled through the ducts from my store to the *Santa Maria* and collected the package from near the tank, where I'd left it."

"You used Lisa," Liz said angrily. "You fed her a line just to get a smuggling route into the *Santa Maria*. What a creep."

"Blame it on that fool, McAndrews. I was all set to marry into a California fortune when he blew in from the great white north. He used his money to impress her with roses and fancy dinners, so she married him. That's women for you."

"And you're a great example of a man."

"Shut up, kid." Christopher pulled against his

handcuffs, trying to force them open. "You think I should respect a woman who dumped me?"

"What about Carroll?" Liz said. "How'd you use her?"

The man laughed. "That poor girl! Her old man's fling with wealth left her so lonely. She tried to get him to pay attention but all he could think about was this mall. Maybe he'll be different now, but I doubt it."

"It sounds to me," Inspector Winter Eagle said, "like you almost care for her. I'm surprised you're capable of such emotions, but it certainly didn't keep you from plotting to kill her father."

"I wanted to destroy McAndrews and his businesses, so I flew up here and got a job as a tour guide. That was the perfect way to learn all the secret details of how the mall worked. At night I stayed late in the office to study the blueprints."

"So you could figure out how to use the air conditioning ducts to get from the *Santa Maria* to any place in the mall?"

"That's right. I took the first bomb through the ducts to the Café Orleans. I hid it on the balcony, then phoned in an anonymous tip after I'd dropped from the air-conditioning duct into the storage room of my store."

"Why the bomb at Full Fathom Down?"

"To set up Benn Dunn as the bomber."

"And the waterpark bomb?"

"If those stupid kids hadn't found it, the blast near the volleyball court would have kept you cops busy while the other bombs were exploding."

"The ones attached to the shark tank and the *Santa Maria*?"

"Yeah. I planted them last night."

"At the hockey game you deliberately acted strangely so the kids would follow you and find the skate bomb. Right?"

He nodded. "I wanted you to suspect Benn Dunn. That's why I put the initials B. D. inside the skate. As soon as the store closed I knocked him out and hauled him through the ducts to the *Santa Maria*. I knew you cops would search his apartment and eventually find the wire I hid between the sofa cushions. It was the same wire used in all the bombs, so Dunn would have looked real guilty. Especially since I knew he'd spent time in prison. Then, after the sharks killed McAndrews, Dunn's body would have been found blown apart, apparently because of an accident in his secret bomb headquarters. The case would have been closed."

"Meanwhile, where would you be?"

"As the sharks enjoyed their snack I'd have crawled through the ducts to my store. Looking all nice and respectable, I'd be establishing my alibi while that creepy little clerk met the death he deserved."

Tom snorted. "I know why you hated Benn Dunn. At the store I remember your face turned white when he refused your order to obey the police. You didn't like him standing up to you, so I bet you enjoyed setting him up as a suspect when you faked that underwater attack. You cut the air hose yourself! That was a dirty trick."

As a police officer took Christopher's arm to lead him away he shook his handcuffs again. "I hate these things," he snarled.

The officer laughed. "You'd better get used to being locked up. You're going to be in prison for a long time."

When Christopher was gone, Liz looked around the mall. "It'll be a different place without those code reds sounding."

Tom snapped his fingers. "Code Red at the Super-mall! How's that for a title?"

"Let's go ask what he thinks." Leaving the *Santa Maria*, Tom and Liz walked over to a crowd of people watching from behind police lines. "Excuse me," Liz said to a man in glasses who was making notes. "Have you picked a title for your new mystery?"

"Not yet! Got a suggestion?" He wrote Tom's idea in his notebook, then took a final picture of them. "So long," he said, shaking hands. "Thanks for your help!"

"You're welcome," Tom replied.

"It was fun," Liz added. "I'll keep my fingers crossed that your book sells a million."

The man laughed. "Wouldn't that be great?"

12

Festival Supermall!

Banners announced the gala event in huge letters. They hung outside stores, across corridors, everywhere above the crowds jamming the mall to celebrate the capture of Christopher Dixon.

One of the biggest banners was at the waterpark, where crowds of kids cheered each blast announcing *surf's up!* Free during the festival, the waterpark was bedlam with laughter, and music from big speakers.

Dietmar Oban continued to defeat all challengers on the Sky Screamer. Watching from below, Tom and Liz saw Dietmar drop from nine stories beside the current second-best, Neil Raj Gill. The challenger fell as swiftly as a barrel over Niagara Falls, but it still wasn't fast enough.

"He's won again!"

Dietmar swam across the splash-down pool, grinning happily. "I'm taking up a petition," he said, climbing out. "This waterslide should be called the Dietmar Drop."

"With your luck it'll probably happen," Tom muttered.

Later he and Liz left the waterpark with Neil Raj, who had invited them to visit Luggage Unlimited during the celebrations. "One of the big festival events is the cooking of traditional foods from other countries. I'm making my famous curry. You've got to try some."

"We'll be there for sure."

The corridors were jammed with tourists, shoppers and sensation-seekers. Clowns performing tricks passed among the people, and a juggler twirled flashing blades. Elsewhere, a woman coaxed her parrot to speak in three languages, while her husband's seal played notes on rubber horns.

Enjoying themselves enormously, Tom and Liz were trying on sombreros at a brightly decorated cart when their parents came out of the crowd. "We're going to Full Fathom Down," Mr. Austen said. "Carroll is giving us a scuba lesson in the indoor sea. Come and say goodbye to her."

"I wish tomorrow would never come," Tom said sadly. "This place is a total adventure."

Benn Dunn was the new manager of the scuba shop, and he looked a lot happier. "I never got along with that guy Dixon," he said to the Austens. "It's thanks to you kids I'm still alive."

Just then Carroll appeared from the storage room. She, too, seemed happier. "Fooled again by another

Mr. Beautiful! Maybe I should start listening to my father's advice."

"Are you moving back to the Caribbean?"

"Not for a while at least, and maybe not at all. I'd miss him too much."

"Will you be going on the morning sub rides with your Dad?" Liz asked.

"Oh yes. It's really important to him."

"I remember watching you in the sub. You didn't look very happy."

"A little voice inside of me kept saying Christopher was involved with the bombs. It was so depressing. Now I wish I'd said something to the police but I had no proof."

"I did," Liz said. "But I didn't even notice it."

"What do you mean?"

"Well, Christopher told me he'd managed a restaurant near Sea World. Later I learned it's in San Diego, which is where your father stole his bride from a jealous boyfriend."

After saying goodbye to the woman, Tom and Liz hurried through the crowded mall to catch a special dolphin presentation. Those showboat mammals—once again watched by a large and adoring audience—gave a great performance. Afterwards the Austens had a chance to speak to Lisa deVita.

"I'm feeling pretty bad about Christopher," she said, then smiled. "But I still believe in love. Hey, I'm Italian! I was born optimistic."

"I'm glad you weren't ever in any danger," Liz said.

"I guess that was my imagination working over-time." She looked at Tom. "Congratulations on nailing that creep at the luggage store. Did he have anything to do with the bombs?"

Tom shook his head. "No, there was never any connection."

"Well, I'm still glad he was arrested."

Not far away, Mr. McAndrews was one of the people taking passengers on festival submarine rides. Between shifts he came up from the dock. "Hi there, you two." He thanked them again for his safe release, then added, "I'm not proud of losing command of that sub."

"But you never had a chance," Tom said. "When it went into the tunnel you couldn't have known Christopher had come through the air-conditioning duct to wait for you to arrive."

"But to be taken by surprise!"

"What could you have done? He dropped the canister of knock-out gas down the conning tower before you could defend yourself, and you weren't wearing a scuba outfit like he was, so you didn't have the protection of a face mask and air supply."

"I guess you're right. If only I'd known that my daughter had fallen in love with the very man who was my enemy. I still can't believe he followed me from San Diego just to get revenge." Mr. McAndrews turned to greet a group of smiling people who'd come out of the crowd. "Tom and Liz, I'd like you to meet the family who built this mall. Years ago they came to Canada and built a successful business in Montreal before coming west with their vision of a supermall."

"You sure succeeded," Tom said. "On behalf of the world's kids, thanks!"

"I'll second that," Liz said.

As they talked to the friendly family members, Mr. McAndrews said, "Where's your friend Dietmar? He told me he's fond of exotic food, and I've made a special dish for the festival: haggis."

"What's that?"

"A traditional dish of Scotland. The innards of a sheep cooked in the skin of its stomach. Delicious!"

"Well, I don't know. Dietmar will eat anything, but . . ."

"If you see him, extend my special invitation. Of course, both of you are included as well."

"Thanks Mr. McAndrews, but no thanks!"

* * *

Soon after, Tom and Liz went into a store called Lots of Fun Stuff. They made a special purchase, then hurried back to Bourbon Street to hear who'd won the Rock the Mall contest. On the way Dietmar joined them, then they saw Heather's manager, Mr. Sutton.

He was on the edge of the crowd waiting for the announcement, still wearing his old-fashioned suit, but with new shoes. "These are for luck," he explained. "I'm really hoping that Heather wins. I've already booked a studio to make her first record."

"But," Liz said, "didn't you say she's not ready yet?"

"Well, I've had second thoughts. She's a great talent and I can't hold her back. I think Heather may be ready for the big time."

"Terrific!" Liz smiled at him. "Remember when I met you with my mom? You'd been talking to Benn Dunn. I kind of wondered about that after he disappeared."

"Years ago I volunteered to help ex-prisoners. Benn's one of the people I meet on occasion, just to make sure that everything's okay. He was pretty upset when the bomb was discovered in his store, kind of thought he'd be blamed because of his past. But it's all fine now, and he'll make a good manager of the scuba shop."

As several people appeared above, all eyes went to the balcony of the Café Orleans. Inspector Winter Eagle said into a microphone, "This is a perfect place for the contest announcement. The first bomb was discovered here and things looked bad for a while. Now everybody's smiling again, and I'm honoured to have a small part in today's big event." She looked at the others beside her. "The announcement of the winner will be made by someone who's special to us all. I've been asked to introduce him, and it's a real thrill. Ladies and gentlemen, please welcome Cayley Wilson."

As cheers and whistles rang out, the blond hockey star stepped to the microphone. "It's great to be making this announcement! We're all expecting wonderful things from the winner of the contest. Please welcome an Edmonton girl who's on the way to success. Here she is: Heather!"

She stepped out onto the balcony to deafening applause. Her face was radiant as she waved to the crowd, then went to the microphone. "There's lots of people to thank, but one person is very special." Pausing, Heather looked in the direction of Tom and Liz. "His name is Mr. Sutton, and he's the world's greatest manager."

As the crowd applauded, Mr. Sutton smiled at Heather. Then after a trophy had been presented to her, Dietmar turned to leave. "I'm out of here."

"Hold it, Oban," Tom said. "There's a special invitation for you from Mr. McAndrews."

After hearing the details of the haggis feed Dietmar said, "It sounds weird, but I'll chance it. After all, my family name comes from a Scottish town."

"Good luck! I'm glad we're going to McDonald's tonight, not McAndrews."

* * *

Long past midnight, Dietmar lay snoring on his bed. Out for the count, he didn't hear the door open between his room and Tom's. A dark shape stood for a moment, listening with unbelieving ears to the decibel count, then the mystery figure swiftly carried out his mission.

* * *

The next morning Mr. and Mrs. Austen were organizing their suitcases. Tom and Liz had finished their packing and were lounging on the sofa, both reading mysteries. Suddenly the door of the Roman Suite burst open and Dietmar stumbled in.

"*It was the haggis*," he screamed. "I've been destroyed!"

Mr. Austen turned slowly, expecting another of Dietmar's gags, then he stared in horror. "I don't believe my eyes! Why did this boy come with us? He's trouble!"

Dietmar ran to the bathroom mirror. "They're still there! I hoped it was just a nightmare! I don't know how, but that haggis did this to me!" Leaning close to the glass, he stared at the bat tattoos above both eyes, the spiders in bright colours on his cheeks, and the tattoo of a tiny snake coiled on the point of his chin. "I look like a kid born into a motorcycle gang!"

"Just before the first bomb was discovered," Liz said to Dietmar, "I found a place in the mall called Lots of Fun Stuff that features quite an interesting product. Here's my map—maybe you'd better find the store and learn how to end your agony." She glanced at her watch. "But make it quick. We leave for the airport soon."

With a cry the boy ran from the suite, moving even faster than his record-breaking fall down the Dietmar Drop.